TAOS
WINTER

A NOVEL

Dr. Elizabeth Hairston-McBurrows

ISBN 978-1-63885-517-0 (Paperback)
ISBN 978-1-63885-518-7 (Digital)

Covenant Books, Inc.
11661 Hwy 707
Murrells Inlet, SC 29576
www.covenantbooks.com

CHAPTER 1

BLIZZARD

T he snow began falling last night around nine thirty. Mia recalls this because she was extremely restless after having spent Friday afternoon apologizing to Corey Hartman. The clock was in plain sight.

Corey and Mia had been close friends for three years—which felt like six. He had answered her cell when they were at lunch, and the voice on the other end was an ex-male friend who said he was checking up on her, mind you, after a year and a half, no communication—no text, e-mail, call, or personal visit.

Lance Romero was notorious for walking in and out of Mia's life until one day she determined that enough was enough. She asked him to leave her home and not to return. She stressed to him that she no longer wanted to be in a relationship with him. Musing on this conversation, Mia thought, "I need to contact Corey." He had, several days prior to the incident, expressed possibly coming down to Taos before Christmas. She whispered a brief but serious prayer. "Lord, please open Corey's heart to forgive me and make the five-hour drive down from Colorado for Christmas."

*****

Mia had officially met Corey at A Touch of Chocolate coffee shop situated about ten minutes from her office while she was on break from an intensive business meeting hosted by the company where she worked. Coincidentally, Corey had also been in attendance at that very same board meeting, but they had not been formally introduced.

She learned that he was from a very polished and success-ful British family living in Franconia, Germany—a quaint historical town known for its rich beauty and culture—and his stately demeanor was a tell-tale sign of his upbringing.

Corey was disciplined, sharp, and extremely knowl-edgeable about marketing and billion-dollar companies in the oil industry. He was a very distinguished, tall and well-built gentleman, not to mention, handsome. Mr. Hartman had been present at the board meeting to pitch some new software for the marketing department of her company. His pitch was superb; and Mia was smitten.

Following his presentation, Mia slipped out of the boardroom to collect her thoughts before closing the meet-ing. Heart fluttering and feeling flushed, she, in puzzled wonderment, asked herself a flurry of questions: *What just happened in there? Who is this man? What is this?*

Her intense attraction to him was highly unchar-acteristic of her. Considering her strict upbringing with Grannie, she was forbidden as a Navajo to keep company

Navajo no company European

with Europeans or Anglo, as is referenced in the Southwest for the Caucasian ethnicity. Mia didn't understand the reasons for this, but as usual, when Grannie spoke, she listened and didn't question her.

She returned quickly to thank him for his pitch and closed out the meeting. Break time meant coffee with chocolate away from the office. As Mia walked into the frequented coffee shop, she breathed a sigh of relief and welcomed the pleasant aroma of a variety of coffees and chocolates. The line wasn't too long—there were only two people in front of her—so she was able to place her order rather quickly. Stepping up to the counter, she said, "I'll have a latte delight with dark chocolate please."

"Name please," asked the attendant.

She paid the cashier and waited for her order.

Mia couldn't understand why she felt a bit flustered, off and on, since the boardroom experience. Mr. Hartman's presentation had done a number on her. Now as she reached for her order, she somehow clumsily dropped her brown Brahmin handbag, keys falling and contents scattering out of an unzipped bag.

"Allow me," said a gentleman, his hand tenderly brushing against hers as he reached to help retrieve her things. His voice was familiar. It was Mr. Hartman of all people!

The warmth of his touch was an electrifying moment for Mia.

The anxiety she felt before and the bewildering questions were once again flooding her heart and mind.

"Thank you, Mr. Hartman." It was a whisper, as Mia could barely get her words out.

Mia rose to determine what to do next about the mess she had made. The staff cleaned up the coffee spill, and the attendant served her another cup of latte delight—at a table this time. Mr. Hartman joined her and introduced himself; she did the same.

"Nice to officially meet you, Mr. Hartman."

"Please call me Corey."

A quiet moment followed, then Corey gave Mia his card and said, "Dinner soon please." His accent was tantalizing.

"I would be honored."

*****

The timing was great! Corey had days free from work while Mia was at Taos for a three-week break from her high-profile job at a major oil company in Eastern New Mexico. She experienced a bit of nostalgia as she remembered Grannie Yazzie, her grandmother, who she grew up with on the Navajo reservation close to the Four Corners. Mia's parents had been arguing and fighting so much that Mia and her sisters, Melanie and Jessica, were left with Grannie during their teenage years. Grannie taught them how to cook, clean, knit, sew, and also instilled lasting values about being ladylike and demanding respect.

It was a cold, rainy day—Mia remembered clearly—when Grannie had lay in bed waiting for Medicine Man and Prophet to come to her. Grannie Yazzie had sent for them as she had grown weak from a high fever and now felt worse than ever.

Mia didn't like the old Indian ways, nor did she understand them. Medicine Man and Prophet came and talked with Grannie—alone at first, but then included the sisters. Their faces exuded gloom. "It *has* to be *serious*," Mia concluded. They went in and stood by Grannie Yazzie's bed.

"Soon I will go the way of the spirits, but you, Mia, will someday be very educated in books and counting," Grannie said, her voice husky and faint.

She added, with all the strength she could muster, "You will become very rich and marry a man from the Western world, and he will honor you."

Mia recalled a poor life on the reservation, but she loved playing with children and would reach out her arms to them when they would come into their yard. Grannie asked the prophet to make a new name for Mia before her departure. He placed his hand on her and said, "From this day until all of the rest of your days, Mia, you shall be called 'Stands With Arms Open' because you always welcome the heavy-laden, the strangers, and the children."

Medicine Man could not help Grannie, so she blessed both girls, then closed her eyes. Leaving the room without tears but being very sad, they were greatly missing her already.

*****

Recollecting her thoughts, Mia Stands With Arms Open was grateful for Grannie's true words that she was now, several years later, experiencing in her life as the second Vice President of Choice Wells Industries.

The thought of spending Christmas break from the oil company during the winter had been a dream of Mia's for at least three years. The dream was finally being realized. Winter at Taos with plenty of snow was anticipated, but the surprise blizzard was not. This calls for a blanket and more wood for the fireplace, which were strategically located in the living area of the most beautiful and comfortable bed-and-breakfast in Taos.

The Place B&B was one of a kind, with light turquoise paint on the walls, viga ceilings, area rugs, and bay windows to die for. It was just the best place to be. This world-renowned historical inn was more than what she expected when she went online months ago to secure lodging for her Christmas vacation.

The snow was falling consistently, and the sun had barely risen over the Sangre de Cristo Mountains. When Mia looked at the clock that just seemed to be right in her face, she struggled to know if Corey would call or just show up to spend the holidays with her. She had been in Taos for over a week.

This is a moment for a nice hot cup of cocoa, Mia thought. It was six fifty in the morning. She moved gracefully from the beautiful and spacious bay window to the kitchenette area, put on a pot of hot water, then stirred the logs in the fireplace while waiting for the pot of water to steam. The fireplace so reminded her of sweet comforting Grannie Yazzie, who passed over five years ago.

Grannie would bring the sisters by the fireplace at their adobe home on the reservation and tell many stories about the old Indian ways. Mia would listen intently. Grannie always insisted the girls cover their laps with handwoven Navajo blankets. They didn't understand why blankets were needed, but Grannie would say, "You cover now with the blanket in the cold days, so then you walk well in your old days." Good

Sitting by the fireplace brought back many warm memories amidst anxious thoughts about Corey and whether he would pack up his Suburban and brave the trip to Taos. Almost forgetting that he may never return to her, nor speak with her again, it seemed her reflecting upon nostalgic moments eased the discomfort about the relationship a bit.

Mia could just smell the home fries that her grannie would make over the potbelly stove in an iron skillet. She'd boil the sliced potatoes for about fifteen minutes, then drain the water off while placing oil in the iron skillet. How Mia enjoyed watching her prepare those potatoes! Grannie added sliced onions, red peppers and, of course, green chili just before they were completely ready. The sisters ate the potatoes with Grannie's delicious fry bread and some beans. Just before removing them from the iron skillet she added salt, pepper, and garlic powder. "The garlic," she'd say, "helps to keep the pressure down when your heart beats fast."

Hearing the sudden kettle whistling jolted Mia out of her nostalgic moment. She went over to the kitchenette and selected a package of hot chocolate mix. The bed-and-breakfast offered Organo Gold hot chocolate; it is a pleasant mix that tastes so much like her *original* cup she had as a child. *Hmmm,* thought Mia, *I'll have to ask the host how I can find this delectable chocolate packet.*

She then decided to see if a signal might be available on her cell or the TV set. Turning on the TV prompted a bit of fear for a fleeting moment about the weather, but with one click, there was the newscaster with, of course, breaking news. A blizzard had developed and was moving from Denver to New Mexico. Five feet of snow was expected with accumulation already two feet deep. Mia recalled reading an article a few years prior that awakened her awareness of God's creative beauty even in snowflakes and challenged her faith in His awesome power. The article revealed that millions of snowflakes fall during any given snowstorm, each having six points but none with the same design. Her heart considered visiting a church in her hometown, Artesia.

As Mia stood looking out of the window adjacent to the bay window but closer to the fireplace, she paused for a moment and surfed the channel. Raton Pass on I-25 was filled with drifting snow. "Not good," Mia whispered. "If only Corey would just *call*! Could he? Would he?" Restless, she went back to sit in the bay window, a cup of hot chocolate in hand.

Startled by a ring on her cell phone, she saw on the caller ID "Corey Hartman." Mia was so anxious, she gasped inwardly, allowing the phone to continue with its beautiful flute music ringtone. Finally, hitting the accept button, she didn't say hello but simply held the phone to her ear. On the other end of the phone was a "Hello, Mia?" coming through the line with a polished European accent, sounding confident yet compassionate. "Are you there?"

Mia finally was no longer encumbered by her anxiety and said, "Yes, yes, yes, of course. Ah, hello, Corey."

"Yes," he said. "Have you forgotten my voice, Mia? What is going on with you?"

"It's just that," Mia hesitated, "I wasn't sure if I would hear from you again."

A knock at the door threw the moment off. She asked Corey to hold for a moment while clinging to the cell phone, "Good morning, Ms. Stands With Arms Open. Are you okay? The temperature has dropped to about eighteen degrees. I thought perhaps you could use a few more blankets."

The innkeeper was pleasant but extremely nosey, as she peered around briefly to see if anyone else was in the living area.

"Muchas gracias," said Mia, a bit irritated because she was anxious to resume her call with Corey.

In a moment of reflection with cell phone in hand and waiting, wanting to see where this relationship was headed, Mia returned to the bay window with a blanket snuggly wrapped around her and said, "So sorry for the interruption. The innkeeper, Mrs. Garcia, brought blankets."

Corey responded with a reassuring voice, "I am happy to know you reached Taos safely and are comfortable during this blizzard." Corey continued reassuring Mia, saying, "I know it has been difficult for you over the last few weeks, but I needed time to sort things out. I wasn't sure if you might consider rekindling our relationship after experiencing the conflict with Lance's telephone call. You seemed to blush and struggle with what you wanted to do after speaking with him. I am strongly interested in a committed relationship."

Mia, silent and concerned, was listening intently.

"Currently," continued Corey, "I am stranded at the Denver Airport, and I so much would like to spend Christmas with you in Taos, but I will have to watch the weather to see if I can eventually rent a vehicle and drive down—if the roads are open and passable enough, of course. Not an option today, and Christmas is only three days away. Keep warm, and I will be in touch."

Mia sighed. "Okay, I will," she hesitated, "pray for a breakthrough with the weather and favor for." She paused again. "Us." She hung up and wondered if she should have mentioned prayer. *Would it turn him off?* she debated in her heart. *Why did I say that?*

Mia decided to leave those concerns for a moment and prepare for breakfast. Mrs. Garcia would be coming back to her suite anytime now with a lovely tray displaying egg omelet with green chili, spinach, red peppers, sausage, and onions. To add even more color to generate an excellent appetite, strawberries, bananas, sliced oranges, and raisin toast. The breakfast presentations were second to none. Mia felt that she could really enjoy her breakfast because a major concern had been temporarily resolved with Corey.

There was a faint knock at the door as Mia headed to her bedroom to find footsies or a warm pair of socks. The temperature was steadily dropping. "Coming right away," Mia yelled. Mrs. Garcia was always on time with her eight-thirty-in-the-morning breakfast for the entire duration of Mia's stay at The Place B&B.

Mia swiftly moved toward the door in the living area, dropping her beautiful Navajo blanket on the bed.

She opened the door to a most delicious-looking gourmet breakfast. "Time for a hearty breakfast," Mrs. Garcia cheerfully said as she set the tray on the dining table of the spacious suite that Mia was living in during her special time away for the winter.

"Thank you, or should I say, muchas gracias," Mia said with delight.

Mrs. Garcia politely left the suite, tugging at her coat in response to the extreme chill that met her when opening the door, though her suite was enclosed in the house; even the hallway was cold. Before sitting to eat, Mia took a look at the fireplace and realized that the wood was getting a bit low. She quickly thought about the issue and decided to eat breakfast while it was still hot. *Nice,* she thought, as a pot of fresh hot chocolate was on the tray. How she loved hot chocolate.

Mia decided to watch the news once again while enjoying her delicious gourmet breakfast. "Oh my," she said, "hundreds of cars are stranded all along I-25, and many flights have been canceled." She wondered how long Corey had been at the airport, realizing that she didn't ask when they spoke on the phone earlier. "Hmmm," she mused, "he can't really drive here or fly. How is a visit to Taos going to come together?"

The hours drifted into the evening with no opportunity to see a New Mexico sunset, especially against the Sangre de Christo Mountains. Mia rested well, hearing the crackling sound of the fireplace that was slowly burning out. She contemplated asking Mrs. Garcia or whomever might be around for firewood as she knew if she didn't get wood tonight, she might freeze. The central heating was not very helpful. She called the reception desk and inquired. The gentleman who answered the phone was pleasant, helpful, and efficient. Though it was about eight thirty in the evening, he brought up wood and placed it in the fireplace properly. Mia was thankful.

Feeling so grateful, she kneeled down beside her bed after the inn staff left and prayed, "Lord, I don't talk with you as much as I believe I should. I don't really know you well at all, but could you send sunshine and less snow so that Corey can travel to Taos in the next couple of days? Thank you!" She slept.

Mia Stands With Arms Open awakened to sunlight peering through the blinds of her lovely southwestern bedroom. She rolled out of bed and allowed her feet to touch the fox rug. Such a comfy feeling it brought. She had awakened to a bright Sunday morning. Reaching for the radio, her cell phone rang. She checked the clock on the radio for the time, and it was seven forty-five. Feeling frustrated, she cried aloud, "Oh no! Breakfast will be served in forty-five minutes!" Then she remembered that breakfast is served at nine o'clock on Sundays. She fell across the bed with a sigh of relief, while the cell phone kept ringing, then stopped and started again. "No way," she whispered, "not Lance again. *This* I do not need."

Lance Romero had served as a CFO of Choice Wells Industries at Artesia when Mia started working there over eight years ago. They seemed to be meant for each other at the start of the relationship, spending many working hours together as Mia had an executive marketing position which closely aligned with the financial section of the company. They had shared many lunch hours and planned dinner dates. Mia cooked and really enjoyed preparing dishes that she learned from Grannie. Lance was an international traveler who enjoyed all types of food, so eating fry bread and posole (a corn soup) was delightful to him. He enjoyed and engaged in great conversations, especially since he and Mia worked in related fields, but the drawback was Lance was too aggressive, arrogant, stubborn, and to top it off, possessive. He had begun stalking Mia within a year of the relationship, going by her condo uninvited and crashing parties then demanding she leave with him. Eventually, he moved to Dallas and worked at an oil company there. Before her three-week break, she decided that he was not the one and was, potentially, very dangerous.

Mia Stands With Arms Open finally answered the call. "Yes," she answered with authority.

Lance said, "Mia, let's talk. Sorry about how I disrespected you over the last year. Give me another chance. Let's start over?" he pleaded.

Her response was, "Absolutely not. Not now, not *ever*! Please do not call me again. As of now I am blocking you!" She continued, "I thought that I could experience a level of peace when you relocated to Dallas, but you've contacted me again. If you don't stop calling or try to come by the New Mexico office, I will file a restraining order." There was a deep silence on the other end. Mia felt good about being able to exude a strong presence on this hopefully final call with Lance.

Lance finally responded, "Goodbye, Mia."

Mia looked out the bay window after disconnecting the call. She wanted to see how the street was looking since the sun was breaking. "This is a beautiful Sunday morning," she observed. Snow was melting but only from the roof of a few buildings. She was pleased that she had chosen a bed-and-breakfast in the business district's really nice area displaying a bakery, a quaint Thai restaurant, cleaners, coffee shop, and a hair salon. A few people went into the bakery.

The morning seemed to move quickly as Mia ate her gourmet breakfast and surfed for a live-streaming church service. Attending church had not been on her agenda for as far back as she could remember. Required mass attendance was only during elementary school days, but now her focus was changing. She paused. "What if God was really answering my prayer from last night? The sun *did* break through this morning and the temperature is rising, though unexpectedly, according to the meteorologist."

Mia found a channel showing a live service streaming from a church in Santa Fe, New Mexico, about an hour and a half from Taos traveling south. Grateful for live streaming, Mia spoke audibly, "Thank you, God!"

The minister announced the title of the message, "Expect the Unexpected: Ephesians 3:20–21."

Mia reasoned, "I don't know how to locate chapters or sections of the Bible. I don't even *have* a Bible." She had an idea. "I will google it." After a few moments she located a Bible app on her laptop, then continued to listen to the church service.

Something is happening to me! It's almost frightening, thought Mia. *Yet it's making me feel warm and peaceful inside.* "Today," she proclaimed to herself, "I will find more scriptures and watch more services!" She felt God's love.

As the hours fled and night fell, she drifted off to sleep. There were no more phone calls, and no one from the inn's staff came knocking on the door. She slept.

She awakened to Christmas Eve—anxious, no, but with questions, yes. Will Corey make it down to Taos? Mia had a fresh idea. "I will skip the B&B breakfast, dress for the weather, and brave the streets." As she prepared to go out, she called the reception desk to let them know that she would not take breakfast. She then grabbed her knee-high tan-colored moccasins, scarf, fur jacket, and handbag. The bakery had just brought out apple walnut muffins from the oven. Mia ordered two and, for a change, a cup of coffee. Both were extremely delicious. The waitress was very pleasant, and the ambiance was great. The city workers were busy clearing the sidewalks and streets.

She left the bakery feeling elated. In that moment, Corey Hartman called. Her heart fluttered. "Merry Christmas Eve, Ms. Stands With Arms Open! Am I still welcome to spend this special day and Christmas Day with you?"

"Are the roads open? I, um, I'm just trying to catch my thoughts, sorry," Mia replied.

"Yes," Corey answered, "and my flight is boarding in a few minutes. I will fly into Taos Regional Airport. Prefer this over flying my jet."

"Of course, you are welcome," Mia answered energetically, recalling her Navajo name briefly—Stands With Arms Open. "Booking a room may be a challenge, though. It's Christmas Eve!" Mia further relayed.

"No worries!" exclaimed Corey. "I completely understand, and I will handle the room issue."

"This is absolutely amazing, Corey!" exclaimed Mia, as they ended the call.

Mia, overwhelmed at this point, went back to her room to prepare for Corey's arrival, which would be in just a short while. She selected a silk turquoise blouse to wear with a beautiful black maxi skirt. She thought this would be an attractive outfit with her black boots and striking silver jewelry. "Now for the hairstyle, let it go free!" Mia's long black hair came just above her waistline and practically exuded a glow. "I am all set now."

Corey reached Mia's suite a few hours after they spoke. His knock on the door was firm yet gentle at the same time. She opened the door to a very handsome, well-dressed gentleman holding firewood.

"Welcome, Mr. Hartman," she said cheerfully.

"Thought you might need some firewood. When I googled this bed-and-breakfast, I learned that there was a fireplace in the suites." His European accent was so delightful to hear. He placed the wood beside the fireplace, and they embraced. The feeling was intoxicating.

Mia wished time could stand still forever.

Reluctantly they pulled away after a moment. Corey took both of Mia's hands in his and said, "I know how much you love art galleries, so I thought we could visit the

Taos Art Museum at Fechin House and, if time permits, The Harwood Museum of Art."

Her eyes beamed at the thought of going out with him, seeing him, talking to him face-to-face. "Yes," she responded.

"It's Christmas Eve," he said, "let's just enjoy the day shopping at the Taos Plaza and, of course, dining at Lambert's of Taos for sushi."

Mia couldn't believe what was taking place. She had dreamed of this moment but wasn't sure if it would become a reality after the conflict previously with Lance Romero. Truly, she was excited! It looked like things were moving forward.

They went to the Taos Plaza, visited art galleries, ate vegetable rolls and tempura salmon at Lambert's, shopped, and talked.

The hours swiftly went by. They returned to Mia's suite and snuggled up by the fireplace, not speaking much but basking in the idyllic ambiance and listening to Christmas music. The evening was so very special.

Corey left around ten in the evening to get settled at another location. Mia thought, *What will tomorrow bring?* She had high hopes.

Early Christmas morning, Corey returned and asked Mia to go out for breakfast. She responded, "I'd rather eat here," and called the desk around seven fifteen requesting breakfast for two.

"How delightful," said Mrs. Garcia. Breakfast was served in Mia's dining area. The two of them were so excited to share Christmas together. Mia had purchased a leather jacket for Corey but had not presented it yet. She was allowing Corey to take the lead. Just as she decided to get her blanket from the bedroom, he took her hand and pulled her to himself and said softly, "Take a seat on the couch, Mia."

Corey kneeled before Mia, presented her with a three-karat marquise engagement ring and proposed. "Mia Stands With Arms Open, will you marry me?" It felt like a warm wind blew throughout the room.

It took Mia a minute, but when the reality of the moment hit, she excitedly embraced Corey. "Yes, Corey, yes! I would marry you!" She composed herself. "Corey Hartman, I would be honored."

*****

The day was only beginning yet felt completed as Mia reflected upon the blizzard, delays, and now sunrise. A new life was beginning for her. If only Grannie could have been with her at this time in her life to see the fulfillment of her desires for Mia Stands With Arms Open.

CHAPTER 2

CHRISTMAS DAY

This was her best Christmas ever! Getting engaged was a dream for Mia that Grannie held very close to her heart, while she, throughout the years, so often wondered if marrying and having babies would work for her. She was so very career-oriented. She fought and pressed to prove that she could become as successful as the medical doctors, professors, congressmen and women that she had so often either seen on television via the news or read about. The reservation didn't give much hope of success to anyone growing up in the '80s, so Mia and her sisters were really proud to know that their great-grandfather defied the odds and became a Navajo code talker during World War II—a great accomplishment in those days. However, Mia was determined that she would not become a prisoner of the Res (short for reservation).

Now on Christmas Day, she was faced with a pleasant challenge. Saying yes to Corey was unexpected yet welcomed.

During the years growing up with Grannie Yazzie, she often spoke to her, Melanie, and Jessica about being good girls. This meant not going out with boys and definitely not getting pregnant! They never asked questions or argued with her to defend themselves. They just listened.

The boys on the reservation all thought that she and her sisters were mean and stuck-up. They were not. They just didn't know how to communicate with them.

Grannie would say, "After you get good grades and finish your schooling, you must go to college and get really good jobs." She and her sisters would giggle about her words at night when Grannie thought they were sleeping. They would cover up their heads with the colorful warm blankets in the winter nights and mock what Grannie had said, in the closest imitation of her voice as they can. "Finish your schooling and go to college." These aspirations seemed impossible to them as Native girls. College? Good jobs? About as far-fetched as flying to the moon!

But they had ambitions of their own. Jessica would say, "I am going to marry a rich, handsome man and have five children." Melanie was always quiet. The only time she seemed to enjoy their times together was when they played jacks, a game in which they would throw a ball in the air and pick up a rock (they couldn't afford the real jacks) before catching the ball. She also loved playing double-Dutch jump rope. Again, they didn't have the real thing, so they improvised. For rope, they would use old cords that they would see lying around dumpsters or in their neighborhood yards. It worked just as well, or at least, they thought so.

Melanie could really determine the flow of the ropes and jump in just in time without missing a beat and continue jumping for at least thirty minutes. She was great in sports, even in school. They all thought she would someday get a scholarship to run track; she was *that* good! But she eventually became friends with a girl who was her classmate. They started hanging out together, getting high on drugs, and eventually stealing. She made the mistake and joined up with bad company, and all dreams of her making it big in sports were shattered.

Mia remember how broken Grannie was the day that the police came to their house looking for Melanie. They never saw her again. They looked for her every day for about two months. Later, they were told that she had spent some time in juve (juvenile detention), then two years later, she overdosed on heroin. They were grief-stricken.

After this, Grannie Yazzie spoke to Jessica and Mia very seriously and said, "You must learn to pray and look after one another. You must study good at school so that you will be okay."

They had never seen or heard Grannie pray and they never went to mass, so they had *no clue* what she was talking about.

Looking back now at those sad days on the Res, Mia couldn't believe how prayer now was a part of her life. Wanting to know more about the Bible and Jesus at thirty-three years of age...unbelievable!

Not only had she recently accepted Jesus into her life, but she had received an engagement ring from the man that she loves on Christmas Day.

*****

The newly engaged Mia pondered, "What are Corey and I going to do to celebrate our engagement? Feast on a lovely meal?" It being Christmas Day added to the jubilation of the moment. "This calls for a special dinner," Mia felt.

Around eleven in the morning, Corey came over to spend the day with her. She had gotten him a nice beige leather jacket and scarf as his Christmas gift. She wasn't sure if it was enough because he was meticulous, but she loved it; hopefully, he did too. Its beige colors along with red and browns were very special. She thought, *Well...I presented it anyway.*

As they sat by the fireplace, she handed him the beautifully wrapped gift box garnished with a red bow. "Merry Christmas, Corey."

He was elated. He said, "Perfect to go with my camel cashmere coat, Mia. I love it." She was relieved.

Now the task of finding a restaurant for dinner. Corey took upon the task of searching the Internet for just the right place for Christmas dinner, considering the fact that some restaurants would be closed on Christmas Day.

As he browsed through the listings, it appeared that a restaurant The Love Apple might be ideal. According to the reviews and photos, it boasted a quaint, romantic atmosphere, which would be a perfect fit for a very special newly engaged couple. The time of service noted on the website indicated an afternoon opening time. "Perfect," he whispered.

Corey was drawn to The Love Apple because it reminded him of his charming, historical, and picturesque hometown of Franconia, Germany, that traditionally bustled with holiday sounds and displayed beautiful decorations at this time of the year. He was usually in awe of it, though Corey's family did not embrace the Christmas celebration as many traditional Christians do, because he actually was born into a German Jewish family. Mia was not aware of this. He wasn't sure if it would matter to her. Corey recognized and respected the Jewish feast days but never really attended synagogues very much. He, however, did take special note of Hanukkah during this celebratory time of the year.

His thoughts trailed back to the restaurant, as he decided to surprise Mia with his choice. The Love Apple it would be. Love had found its way into both of their hearts.

Mia was extremely excited to go out later in the afternoon to a special restaurant that Corey had carefully and intentionally selected for their Christmas dinner.

Time had flown by on this special day so quickly. It was enjoyable.

Corey went back to his lodging around four in the afternoon to freshen up for their dinner date. There was music playing from one of the stores on the street. *"Hark the Herald Angels Sing" sounds especially lovely today*, Corey thought as he walked another short block with a skip in his step.

*****

A few people were scurrying about with shopping bags in hand, wearing fur or leather gloves, with boots and caps. Seriously, the weather was inclement.

Corey didn't make a fuss about what to wear; he just needed to change sweaters, he thought, and gargle a bit to protect himself against colds and flu and, of course, to feel more refreshed. Corey didn't bother about his looks of blown curls. They had a mind of their own, if you will, plus he was planning to put his cowboy hat on for the evening. Grabbing his keys and turning out the lights, he reflected, "Whether this is Christmas or Hanukkah, I am delighted to celebrate it with a very special lady whom I have fallen deeply in love with—Stands With Arms Open.

While Corey was heading back to Mia's lodging place, she thought of her sister Jessica, whom she had not spoken with or heard from in months. Looking through her address book, she happened upon Jessica's number. Mia dialed the number immediately.

"Hello, Jessica," Mia said.

"Seriously, Mia, it has been over six months since you have called me!" Jessica exuded annoyance.

"I have tried many times to reach you, but what do I get? Your voicemail."

"Why now?" asked Jessica.

"I was thinking that I need to keep in touch with you more, especially now that Melanie is gone," Mia said cautiously.

"This is true, but it never happens!" Jessica spoke roughly. "You are rich and educated; I still struggle. It won't work. You don't have time for me. You have your friends that are equal with you. It's just—"

A knock on the door interrupted Mia's conversation. Jessica didn't finish her sentence as Mia interrupted her and said, "I'll call you back."

Jessica hung up without a goodbye. Mia didn't blame her sister for being upset.

As Mia went to the door, she noticed that Corey was on his cell. She motioned for him to come in as he closed out his conversation with Best Limo of Taos. "Sure," he said, "five thirty is fine." He had ordered a luxury sedan to pick them up for dinner. He felt good about having made this decision as he walked out of his bed-and-breakfast earlier.

Corey sat for a moment as Mia finished selecting her jewelry and putting on her suede Native-style light brown moccasins.

Another knock at the door indicated that the driver had arrived. Mia was so elated as they walked outside. Closing the door behind them, she said, "Amazing, Corey. You are simply amazing!"

The drive was pleasant as they observed a few people out; some holding hands, others trying to keep their composure while walking on snowy, slushy sidewalks and streets.

The sounds of bells ringing and the music playing on the radio in the limo set a romantic stage that could not be expressed in words. Corey placed his hands on Mia's as they rode past decorated buildings and homes. Staring deeply into her eyes, Corey said, "Stands With Arms Open, you are my love, my dream come true."

Mia leaned over a bit toward Corey as her beautiful long shiny hair fell over the side of her face and said in a hushed tone, "I don't know how to say what I feel at this moment." She pulled back slightly.

Corey responded, "You don't have to say anything."

After about a fifteen-minute drive, they had arrived at The Love Apple restaurant. *Lovely*, thought Mia. *What an excellent choice.* She carefully observed the Spanish architecture and quaint designs that somehow reflected an old chapel. "Corey!" she exclaimed. "How did you find this place?"

"The Internet," he responded with confidence and excitement.

"The Internet, of course."

As they disembarked from the car, Corey spoke a brief word to the driver, then came around to the passenger's side to escort Mia into the restaurant.

There were several couples seated in an outdoor patio area, irregardless to the cold of the night. Small fires were lit in the area in an ornate container, which allowed the fire to burn incessantly. "How clever," she spoke loudly, not realizing that her response to the patio setup may have come across as a bit crass to the host who had discreetly approached them. She felt embarassed. The host gave no indication that she had heard the remark.

"Hartman," said Corey to their host. They were then escorted to their seats.

Mia loved the ambiance, not only the quaintness but the comforting feel of the place, the warmth and the inviting atmosphere that it exuded. "Corey, I love this place," she quietly whispered in his hearing.

He smiled and nodded. "Yes."

The servers were neatly attired in black-and-white combination uniforms, well groomed, and very pleasant. The Love Apple restaurant is considerably new French Mexican fusion. When they arrived, fresh-baked stone-ground blue cornbread with maple walnut butter was brought out to their table. They first ordered an appetizer of Chanterelle mushrooms, then Mia ordered ruby trout and gnocchi Italian potato dumpling. Corey hesitated and then said, "I will have the antelope, lightly seared, with scalloped potatoes."

"Hmm…antelope? What does that taste like?" Mia was curious to know.

Corey replied, "A lot like…antelope!" He laughed out loud.

Mia was slightly taken aback because she never expected antelope to be on the menu. Her experience with antelope was what she recalled her grannie speak of as an animal which you cannot cook unless you know *exactly* what you are doing. They can stink something awful.

The food was beyond delicious; it was delectable with awesome presentations. This was a dining experience to be remembered throughout the years to come. Mia did not want the experience to end, but after dessert—chocolate croissants and a cup of coffee for her and some cheesecake for Corey—he motioned to the server that he was ready for the check. Retrieving his American Express card carefully from his wallet, he placed it in the check folder and clasped together his hands and placed them on the table and said, "This was a very special night, Mia. I was thinking—"

The server returned with the check folder, card inserted of course. "Here you are, sir," the server said, handing the card with one hand, with the other behind his back. Corey reached into his bill folder again, replacing the card and pulling out a crisp one-hundred-dollar bill, and gave it to the server.

"Sir, I am most grateful."

Silence for a moment was followed by chairs being pushed back from the table. Corey signaled with his hand for Mia to wait. He moved around to her side of the table and said, "Please allow me."

For a moment she was a bit embarassed thinking that she should have known to wait. Stands With Arms Open knew how to be hospitable on the reservation as a child, and she knew how to make guests feel welcome at the office and her home but had very little experience regarding courtesies or expectations when in a gentleman's company. Opening car doors for her was different, and especially waiting for him to assist with seating and rising from her chair was all new to her.

Grannie Yazzie never talked to her and her sisters about etiquette, only many admonishments about schooling and staying away from boys. How she missed her grannie, to say the least.

*****

Corey and Mia exited the lovely restaurant, and they both took one last glance back. The Spanish archways spoke very clearly to them both that this would be a perfect place for a private wedding but kept their thoughts to themselves.

How did the driver know to return at this time? Mia mused.

Surprisingly, Corey answered her question without even hearing her thoughts. "I gave him an approximate time that we would need him back here." He just seemed to know what Mia was thinking. She just nodded a yes.

As they rode back to the bed-and-breakfast, Corey asked Mia if she wanted a bottle of water that was situated in a special water beverage holder in the back of the seats in front of them.

"No, thank you," Mia said.

"Are you well, Mia?" Corey asked. "You seem a little distant since dinner?"

"I am well," she responded softly. "I don't want the evening to end. It has been such an extraordinary day, I just don't want it to end," she repeated.

"Do you want me to stay for the night with you? We can roast marshmallows and sit by the fireplace listening to Christmas music. I know how much you like Christmas!" He began to recall that he had never shared with her about his Jewish roots.

"I *do* like roasting marshmallows and Christmas music. It brought us so much joy growing up on the reservation. We looked forward to it all year. But by the end of the day we were sad again—so superficial was our joy. But being with you today, Corey, has been *super-special!*"

The sentiment was mutual. Mia stopped speaking, and Corey took that opportunity to share about his Jewish background with her. He felt she needed to know.

"Mia," he reluctantly spoke, "I normally do not celebrate Christmas. My family…well…I am a German, but I am also Jewish." He turned his head away for a moment to look out of the car window. He was frustrated because he didn't know what to say or do next. Turning back toward Mia, he took both her hands and said, "I have never accepted Christ in my life as I hear is the way to become a Christian. Many people have approached me through the years, including some who claim to be Messianic Jews. I just don't know what to do moving forward, but I am open now. What are you thinking at this moment, Stands With Arms Open? Are you open to share with me about your faith?" Mia was silent.

He trailed on, trying to explain, "I mean, I don't really attend synagogue unless I am home with my parents. I have thought of attending a few times since I've been living in Colorado Springs and even contemplated purchasing a Bible, but I have not gotten around to it as yet."

Mia finally broke her silence. "I don't have a Bible either, Corey. I just recently began to have an interest in who Jesus is since I have been here during my holiday leave."

"Go on," Corey said.

Though they were engaged, they were only now opening up to each other about themselves.

"Well, you see, I grew up on a reservation in the Four Corners of New Mexico, you know the place?"

"No," he said. "I only know of them from reading tourism brochures."

Okay, she thought, *here goes.* "Are you aware I am Navajo?"

"No. I knew you were a First Nations people, but not specifically Navajo, and I really don't know your culture. But similar to my curiosity about being a Christian, I am open. Go on and speak freely, Mia. I am in love with you, and I want to spend the rest of my life with you." She began to weep. "Please talk to me, dear. I want to understand," Corey said tenderly.

Mia decided it was time to let him all the way in.

"Okay," she began with a heavy sigh. "My Grannie Yazzie watched over me and my sister Melanie, who died of an overdose of heroin a few years ago."

"Sorry, Mia. Truly sorry," said Corey.

"It is sad for me. Nevertheless, my sister Jessica is living…I believe in Arizona. I know how this sounds, but," Mia paused, trying to contain herself. "To continue," she related, "Grannie practiced old Indian ways and would take us to the Catholic Church on the res, but they never really spoke or taught us about Christ. The center of that entire experience was baby Jesus and Mary, His mother.

"We attended special feast days for Christmas time, fall, and summer. I myself want to know more about Jesus Christ. Something about Him interests me. When I attended college (Grannie's dream for all three of us) at the University of New Mexico, there were student evangelists there who would come to me saying and sometimes singing—"

Mia found it hard to go on. The memory brought about a torrent of tears. Corey assured her too that it was okay to share her heart.

Mia pressed on. "They always said that God had a plan for my life, and I would feel very warm inside when I would hear this, but I would never stop to take it all in. I would continue walking away swiftly or rebuff what they said because it frightened me a lot.

"But a few days before you arrived I knelt by my bed and asked Jesus to help me to know Him better. Since then, I've watched ministers on my laptop livestreaming, and I really believe that Jesus has touched my heart."

"Can we share together before I leave for Colorado Springs in a couple days?"

"Yes," Mia ecstatically answered, "let's do that!"

The limo driver pulled up to the bed-and-breakfast. They thanked him and headed to the door. "Would you like to come in for a few minutes, Corey?"

"Yes," he said, "it is still a bit early."

She asked him to excuse her for a moment to remove her sueded native boots. This was always a hassle for Mia, but she loved them. So many laces and difficulty pulling them off her feet. Just as she headed down the hallway, they both heard an extremely loud crash. Corey called for Mia, but there was no answer.

Oh my, Corey thought, *did someone shoot through a window?* Corey was concerned for Mia. *Was she hurt? Why didn't she answer me?*

She had fainted in the hallway.

He didn't see the tree fall through a window in a room to the side of the living area. Where he was sitting was not affected. He dashed to the hallway, where he found Mia lying on the floor. He was perplexed as to what had happened.

Leaning over to check Mia's pulse, he was relieved that it was good. He didn't want to leave her side but needed to get help. The dilemma was mind-boggling. There was no blood. Corey breathed deeply and thought, *Good, but now what?* He checked around the kitchen area to see if there was an emergency number on the fridge or counter for the bed-and-breakfast. He found it. He picked up the phone to call, but there was no dial tone. "This is just great!" he exclaimed sarcastically, disappointed.

The line may be down, he concluded, as he recalled on the way back from dinner that the wind was picking up and there were a few consistent flurries. He didn't think too seriously about the wind at that time; after all, this was Taos, New Mexico, in mid-December. He later found out that a large tree trunk had fallen onto the window of this beautiful lodging place and took out the phone lines with it. He thought to himself, *What are the chances?*

He needed to get help for Mia. "Think, Corey," he whispered to himself desperately. He checked his phone and realized that cell communication had not been disrupted by the fallen tree. "Okay, I will call the EMT and the fire department."

Time to check on Mia again. She was still unconscious.

Let me see, should I move her to her bed? No. I think the EMTs would need to determine that. Corey's mind was a flood of unclear thoughts.

Calm down, Corey! It will be okay!

Whose voice am I hearing? he wondered, looking around the room to see if someone else had entered. There was no one. *Who said that?* It was baffling, to say the least.

The sound of roaring sirens of the approaching fire truck and ambulance gave Corey the needed break from the mysterious voice he is *sure* he imagined. The emergency vehicles had arrived.

"Awesome!" Corey spoke loudly. He quickly dashed to the door to welcome them.

Coming into the suite, one of the fire rescue personnel asked, "What do we have here?" From the outside of the building he had seen that a large Christmas tree had fallen through the window, and now he glanced at Mia on the floor and had a fleeting thought that this was also a domestic violence situation.

Corey, immediately discerning what the officer was thinking, responded confidently, "This is not what you are thinking. We just returned from a special dinner to celebrate our engagement, and my fiancée went down the hall to go to her bedroom. I was sitting in the living area waiting on her, when I heard a loud crash. I came running to see if she was okay, and I found her lying here. I don't know what happened!"

The EMTs checked her vitals while the firemen assessed the broken window and tree issue. They confirmed that it was in fact the wind's intensity—which by now was blow-ing at up to 35 to 40 mph—that had caused the damage. The fire chief did an assessment and reported, "The tree looks like a Nordic Spruce species. I'd say, almost sixty feet in height and close to thirty feet wide. That's a huge one. Lots of trees like these in Taos, and they are popular during this season."

Making a decision to move Mia to a gurney, one of the attendants placed smelling salts under her nose. The pungent smell jolted her back to reality. She opened her eyes. Startled by all the attention, naturally, she inquired, "What happened, Corey? What is going on?"

"You will be fine," responded the head of the team. "You apparently fainted," he said, glaring at Corey. He was still suspicious. "A drink of water and rest would be the best thing for you for now."

"A large tree fell through one of your windows and, of course, broke it, so that is what you heard."

Mia was still a bit dazed. "What is this really all about? I don't understand."

Corey assured her that all would be well. He held the *voice* experience in his heart until they were alone—the voice that spoke to him.

"We did some clearing out of glass and debris and covered the window temporarily until the innkeeper can repair it properly," declared one of the firemen.

They left, saying a loud "Merry Christmas!" to them before walking out the door.

The EMTs stayed behind a little longer, ensuring that Mia's vitals were stable. They emphasized again, "She needs a glass of water and just a time of rest."

"Okay, you guys take care now," the medical personnel said, as they too prepared to go.

By now they had moved Mia to her bed. Corey saw them out and stopped for a moment to say thank you. He wondered if God was speaking to him earlier. He quickly shrugged that notion off and swiftly returned to Mia. He found her alert and sitting up.

"Take it easy, Mia," Corey said with concern, embracing her. Then, without warning, their eyes locked and it felt like the world stood still. Something electric was taking place between them. They both sensed it. He held her passionately. She began to weep, for this was a moment of moments. She forgot about the tree, the world, people—everything faded away from her mind as she found herself lost in Corey's arms.

What do I do now? she questioned. *I am afraid, but I don't want to say no.* He didn't speak. She became silent and continued weeping. *I wanted to wait until my wedding night,* she argued with herself, *yet everything is changing in this moment.* She relented.

The night passed and the sun had just begun to rise. Corey got out of bed before Mia awoke and went to the living area and laid down on the couch. His mind was filled with thoughts of *last night,* so he could not fall back to sleep. He struggled with what their hearts felt and was concerned about the journey ahead. He knew that the conflict he was somehow feeling would not be easy to make sense of. It was unsettling to him. He decided to get up and prepare some hot chocolate.

When Mia eventually awakened, she came to the realization of what had taken place.

Convicted, she slid out of bed and laid on the Moroccan rug and prayed, "Jesus, please, *please*, forgive me. I have never known much about what is right or wrong before you, but I know without a shadow of a doubt that what happened last night was not right and I am sorry. Please help me, Lord. Live in my heart from today and always. I am so ashamed. Please help me. Forgive me."

At the same time, while Corey was in the kitchen preparing the hot chocolate, he was having his own spiritual experience. He heard the mysterious voice again, boldly this time, with a slight echo saying, "Corey Hartman!"

He felt a jolt and turned around to see who had called his name. It sounded like the voice he had heard earlier in the evening. *What is this mystery? Could it be—?* He got his answer.

"I am the God of Abraham, Isaac, and Jacob. Jesus Christ is the Messiah. Learn of Him!"

CHAPTER 3

THE DAY AFTER

Corey determined that he would seek clarity about the voice which spoke to him twice in one day. This was an experience that he had heard about when attending synagogue a couple of times while the rabbi taught, but who was *he* to have such a spiritual experience?

"Later—" he contemplated, being interrupted by a knock at the door. Opening the door there was someone who appeared to be a maintenance person.

"Good morning," said Corey.

"Oh, pardon me," the gentleman replied. "Looks like there must have been a bit of excitement yesterday, eh?"

Corey responded with a puzzled look, "Pardon me?"

"Sorry," the maintenance guy said. "My name is David. I am here to assess the damage from last night."

"Very well," answered Corey, "go right ahead."

In the meantime, he checked to see if Mia wanted some hot chocolate as well. She was stretched out by now on the beautifully designed Moroccan rug, covered in a red and turquoise Navajo blanket, *praying*. Corey quietly excused himself without saying a word.

David was repairing the lounge area of the room that had been damaged from the fallen tree on Christmas night.

"Wow, good thing that there were no lights on that tree. Looks like it was the only one that had a small amount of decorations."

Corey moved toward the bedroom again to see if Mia was available to talk with him. By now, she was walking out of the room and inquired, "Who is in the front room?"

"The maintenance guy, David."

"Was he able to replace the window?"

"Yes," answered Corey.

During all of the commotion, Mrs. Garcia had come by also to check on the window and to make sure Mia was okay. She also gave Mia some paperwork to complete regarding the incident and asked if she wanted breakfast.

"Sure," responded Mia. "Could you please provide an additional breakfast for my guest, Mr. Hartman?"

"Sure thing, Mia," answered Mrs. Garcia.

David gathered his tools and waved goodbye as though he was in a big rush. No one responded.

"How are you feeling, Mia?" asked Corey, speaking a little reluctantly to her because he didn't understand her previous posture when he went to check on her earlier, wrapped in her Navajo blanket, weeping. He didn't know that she was communicating with Christ the best way that she knew. There had been no one in her life to lead her to the Lord, teach her the Word of God, and help her to develop a prayer life. "The voice that I heard, I wonder—"

Mia interrupted, "Corey, I am fine, but what about you? Are you okay?"

"Yes, yes, Mia. Let's just say I *will* be okay."

She was concerned now. Last night, what they did was wrong, bad timing, inappropriate, but she loved Corey deeply.

There was another rap at the door. Mrs. Garcia came in with two lovely breakfast trays displaying Canadian bacon, boiled eggs, pears with shredded Brie cheese, and cinnamon rolls with icing. In addition, they were served coffee and chilled grapefruit juice.

They enjoyed breakfast in the midst of silence. Neither of them knew what to say. Mia reflected on her time talking with the Lord, while Corey struggled with understanding the message he received from a mysterious voice.

"More coffee?"

Mia nodded to Corey. "Just a bit, thank you."

While he poured the coffee he built up the courage to ask, "Do you still want to marry me?"

She avoided the question and instead decided to apologize.

"I am really sorry about last night, Corey. I knew that I should not have been intimate with you. My Grannie Yazzie warned me and my sisters against this years ago. Not that it was the first time being sexually involved. I grew up being molested by my father and hated every moment— the shame, the guilt, and the fear of being exploited. I have had counselling for this issue, but I stopped going to my appointments. It was like reliving the trauma over and over again.

"The counselors that were assigned to me during my junior year at high school made me feel that the molestation was all my fault. The principal of my school on the reservation called me into his office several times due to my lethargic behavior and low grades after having been a straight-A student from my freshman year. The first thought that comes to the mind of my teacher or principal in the Navajo community is that of alcoholic abuse. At that point I had not—nor have I since—*ever* drank alcoholic drinks. My mom and dad were alcoholics, and I determined that I would *never* be like them. I—"

Corey interrupted by placing his hand on hers, saying, "Did you ever speak with anyone else about what you were experiencing? Your grannie? A friend?"

"Corey, that was not realistic for me nor my sisters. I had no friends. I would *never* have told Grannie Yazzie. That would have been a big mistake. You see, fear gripped me for years. I was miserable and didn't know how to go on…but I managed."

Corey listened to her every word, feeling Mia's pain, yet for a moment he appeared caught up in his own world of distant memories.

She continued. "We had two distinctly different upbringings, Corey. It was only when I went to college that I began to learn how to communicate what I was feeling and understand that I was not at fault. I had a professor who, I didn't realize at the time, knew the Lord very much. She called me into her office several times in my freshman year and began to just talk with me and encourage me. She was my African American Heritage professor. I was interested in this course, so I took it as an elective. My major was Chemical Engineering, and I minored in Economics. This course with Dr. Lorina Jackson changed my life because she was sensitive to my situation and she spoke hope over me. She would say, 'Mia Yazzie, you will accomplish greatness in your life. Your destiny is filled with prosperity.'

"She never said, 'You need to go to church' or 'You need to ask God to forgive you.' She would just say those inspiring words to me each time we spoke in her office. Today, I am thankful."

By now they were finished with breakfast, so Corey pushed back from the table and said, "Let's just make today a rest day, mainly for you. You should rest. Last night was a bit too much for you, with the tree falling in the window and your anxiety attack and, well, you know what else… don't you, Mia?"

"Yes of course, Corey," she reluctantly answered.

"At any rate, I have several proposals to look over for my company, so I will excuse myself and check on you later, okay?" He leaned over, kissed her on the cheek, and started gathering his coat, scarf, hat, and gloves. "I will see myself out."

The room became unusually still after Corey left.

Tears welled up in Mia's eyes, then began to stream down her face, silently at first, and then she began to weep uncontrollably.

"What have I done? I have just lost the love of my life!" She was sure of it!

Stands With Arms Open eventually drifted off to sleep on a wet pillow due to the deluge of tears shed.

Around six in the morning, she was awakened by her cell phone ringing. She thought, *Why didn't I just turn the phone off last night? I need the sleep.* But she reached for it anyway.

"Mia, good morning," the voice on the other end inquired.

"Corey?" she asked, though she knew it was his voice.

"Pack an overnight bag, I am taking you to Santa Fe today. I believe a change of scenery would be good for the both of us. Sorry about leaving abruptly last night. Just needed to process what you shared about your past experiences. Say yes. We could leave in a couple of hours…say around eight o'clock? This would allow us to arrive around nine forty-five, just in time to share a nice New Mexican breakfast in a different environment. Have you ever spent any time in Santa Fe, Mia? Touring? Dining?"

"No," she responded with little interest.

"I…I often thought of it," Corey revealed, "but didn't want to go alone. What better person to go with than you?"

Mia's heart fluttered. *Perhaps the relationship is not over after all,* she mused, *but as for staying overnight, I couldn't do that! We have not yet married, and I am still feeling sad about the mistake I made on Christmas night.*

"Corey, can't we return in the evening? I don't want to stay overnight," she replied.

Corey offered a little more detail to settle her mind. "I have arranged for two separate haciendas at Hotel Santa Fe, a lovely quaint hotel not very far from the plaza. You would love it so much."

Mia wondered about the hacienda but didn't remark or ask Corey any more questions. She decided to go and just see what this was all about. She said yes.

CHAPTER 4

SANTA FE

C orey prepared a convenient overnight bag with lots of excitement. For many years living in the Southwest, he enjoyed visiting one of the most intriguing cities in the United States, Santa Fe.

He had first traveled to New Mexico as a child when his grandfather came from Germany as an immigrant and settled in Colorado with his father. His mother eventually came. The Hartmans were astute and determined. Hartman Enterprises was his Grandfather Frank's first business— import and export. It developed quite well.

Throughout the years Corey learned about business management and developed a stern but effective approach to managing business. He later founded Hartman Hydraulics after being inspired about the procedures of supply and demand at the University of Cambridge, United Kingdom.

Between Corey's experiences with his grandfather and university, he knew that he would do well collaborating oil companies with those that produced and operated hydraulic systems.

Now in this special time of his life, December 2017, Corey is excited to spend some quality time in Santa Fe with his fiancée.

He finished his preparations for travel while listening to the radio. The weather report seemed a bit challenging. Six inches of snow was expected as a possible storm was coming down from Colorado in a couple of days. The winds had subsided quite a bit from what they had experienced the night before, but things could change from minute to minute. Corey almost reconsidered travelling to Santa Fe but thought again that two days before the storm would allow enough time to drive down and come back after an overnight stay. He had plans of flying back to Colorado Springs after returning from Santa Fe but had not divulged this bit of information to Mia. It would be a surprise to her, an unwelcome surprise, he was sure.

He began the short walk to Mia's place, thinking, *I should talk to Mia about the voices that I have heard, and I should also let her know about my departure tomorrow afternoon.*

Walking down the street, feeling the cold against his face, Corey noticed that the winds that had subsided seemed to be increasing again.

Reaching Mia's, he knocked as she continued canceling breakfast with Mrs. Garcia over the phone.

"Yes, that is correct. I will not need breakfast tomorrow as well. Thank you so much, Mrs. Garcia. Sorry for the inconvenience." She simultaneously opened the door for Corey and motioned for him to please come in and be seated. He chose to stand and greeted her with a slight hug, then checked the window again that had been replaced.

"Ready, Mia?" he asked.

"Yes, I'm ready. Here's my overnight bag."

He reached for it, then took a moment to quiet Mia and inquired, "How are you, Mia? *Really?*"

"I'm okay, Corey. *Now* I am okay."

He decided not to pursue the conversation any further. Mia looked around the room as if to see if she'd left anything behind. Feeling fairly confident, Corey invited her to head out of the door first. He also looked behind briefly, then motioned for keys to lock the door properly. They headed for his rental SUV that was parked just outside the door of the apartment. Reaching the passenger side, he assisted Mia, then closed the door. As Corey reached the driver's side, Mia's cell phone rang.

"Hello," the voice on the other end said. "Mia, this is Jessica."

Corey felt relieved because he thought briefly that it might have been Lance.

"How are you, Jessica?" Mia did not want to have this conversation with her sister, especially not now!

"Well," sounding anxious, she went on to say, "I am about to get evicted. Can you send me $500 to pay my rent? I know we don't talk much, but I need your help."

Mia Stands With Arms Open was silent, with the phone to her ear. Corey gazed at her as he touched the ignition to start up the vehicle. He wondered to himself, *Where is this conversation going? And just as we were headed out for a nice trip too.* He felt somewhat annoyed at the lack of proper timing of the call.

Mia finally responded to her sister on the other end. "I don't know, Jessica. What will you do about next month, and the next? Where is your friend who was living with you? What are you doing? You shouldn't live with the guy anyway. Respect yourself more than this."

Jessica did not call to get a lecture. "Never mind, Mia. You only think about yourself! I get it. You think you are better than me!" Jessica's voice was rising in volume, and Corey was able to pick up bits and pieces of what she was saying to Mia.

Corey became frustrated because he didn't understand Mia's relationship with her sister. And the call, the conversation, it seemed out of character.

Jessica hung up, and Mia stared blankly at the phone in disbelief.

"Sorry, Corey. That was my sister Jessica."

"I surmised as much," he responded reluctantly.

"I would love to have a good relationship with her at this time of my life, but we are from two different worlds now. As kids growing up, we were very close, but that reality has since long diminished. Our values, our goals are so very different. I don't know, Corey." She felt sad.

He took her hand in his and said, "There are some things that we are unable to control, and this is one of them—"

Mia interrupted him, "She needs money for her rent."

"Do you want to help her?" asked Corey.

"Yes," Mia said, "but it wouldn't really help her. It would be a temporary fix. It's like being on drugs. The problem doesn't get solved with a quick fix."

By now they were headed into New Mexico, 68-South, and eventually connecting to 84-East/US Highway 285-South.

Silence. Driving. Mia nodded off a bit because she had begun to relax after the disturbing call from her sister.

"Do you want to take a nap, Mia?" Corey inquired.

"Oh, I'm sorry, Corey. I'm just a little bit tired," she explained. "Did you want to talk?"

"No, it's okay, Mia. Just rest."

She thought of how she loved this trait of Corey's— very caring and sensitive.

Growing up on the reservation, there were no examples or role models of men showing love and caring for the women. Because of this, she sometimes felt a bit afraid to receive any form of endearment from a man, wondering if there might be some ulterior motive for their actions.

She slept for a bit, awakening to music from the radio as Corey drove down I-25 South. The scenery was fresh and beautiful, and it felt as if it was the first time that she had enjoyed it.

Corey commented that they would soon be entering the Santa Fe City limits.

"How long was I asleep?" she asked groggily, slightly embarrassed. But she heard what Corey had said and was glad they were approaching Santa Fe. "Sounds great," Mia replied.

"Breakfast soon, right, Corey?"

"Yes," he answered, "first thing on the agenda for today."

The music playing on the radio was not exactly distasteful, but Mia longed to hear a song or a sermon from a Christian station. She said nothing.

After about another half an hour, they both saw signs pointing to Santa Fe. They were about to enter into a historic city, which is the oldest capital of the United States and was actually founded in 1607, prior to New Mexico becoming an official state of the United States of America.

It is also known as a "City Different." As far as you can see in the foothills, there are lovely adobe-style homes and businesses. This is Santa Fe.

Corey had chosen Cafe Pasquals for breakfast. Mia was not familiar with the area, nor was she adventurous enough to surf the Internet for a breakfast place.

They drove through the famous plaza square in search of a parking space. This was a challenging task due to the narrow streets congested with lots of traffic. This was especially true during the high-tourist seasons. Corey eventually found an area that might work for parking, though it meant that they would have to walk a bit in the cold and windy atmosphere, but it was still special. Decorations were still in place, and the people on the sidewalks displayed a very friendly attitude. Corey and Mia were considered as a mixed couple in many cultures, but it didn't seem to matter in Santa Fe, or really in New Mexico for that matter. This was a good thing.

New Mexico's demographics is made up mainly of Hispanics, Native Americans, and Anglos, with only about 4 percent African Americans.

They located Cafe Pasquals and were delighted to be welcomed into such an intimate, rustic setting. After about ten minutes they were seated, menu in hand. There was a Navajo family seated next to their table. Mia greeted them.

"Good morning," they responded warmly.

As they perused the menu, Mia remembered Grannie Yazzie. She glanced at the menu then looked up to observe the family that she had just greeted. Memories, so crystal clear.

I should call Jessica after breakfast, Mia thought resolvedly. *After all, she is my only family; there is no one else.*

Corey inquired, "Are you okay? Did you select what you wanted to order?"

"I'm thinking home fries with fried egg and red chili on the side," she said.

The server came over to see what they wanted for drinks. Corey quickly answered, "A hot chocolate for the lady, and I will take a coffee…black."

Strange, thought Mia. *He didn't ask me what I wanted to drink. I suppose I should have spoken up to say I would rather have grapefruit or tea.* She let it go. *Why spoil the moment?* she mused.

During breakfast Corey shared his plans for them. They would visit the Cathedral Basilica of Saint Francis of Assisi. It dates back to 1886.

He also shared with Mia that they would go to see the Miraculous Staircase—both in walking distance. Shopping was on the agenda, depending on how Mia felt about it.

The family that Mia had so quickly become fond of, prepared to leave, pushing the chairs and gathering their belongings. They said, *"Yá'át'ééh abíní."* ("Good morning.")

"Háa, ish ní't'ée?" ("How are you?")

"Jó'yá a t'ée a wee wii siizhį́į." ("Nice to meet you.")

The eldest member of the family, who was perhaps the grandmother, touched Mia on her shoulder on the way out. Stands With Arms Open felt a warm sensation for a moment. Soon after, their breakfast was served, hot and looking delicious. "Here you go. Enjoy."

It was a tasty breakfast in such a pleasant atmosphere. Their server came back often to top up Corey's coffee, perhaps a little too often. Corey would say "I'm fine, thank you" over and over again. Finally, he gave in to the persistent server and said, "Sure," making way for him to pour another fill of the dark liquid. Mia chuckled.

"Anything else for you, dear?" Corey asked.

Hmm. He had never addressed her as dear before. Okay, that's different. "No. I am fine. Thanks, Corey."

When they were finished eating, Corey gathered their belongings and assisted Mia with her coat.

The server returned with the check, which he quickly signed, and continued dressing for the cold weather. The last time he checked the temperature it was twenty-two degrees with a high-windchill factor.

The cathedral was extremely beautiful, and the history of it was equally special. Its architecture is considered as a Romanesque revival style. It is an amazing cathedral.

The next stop was Loretto Chapel. Mia had heard of it a few times before, but now she was getting to see it and experience it in person. She was delighted.

This particular chapel was filled with mystery and wonder. It excited her. Legend has it that a mysterious man showed up at the chapel in 1873 after a prayer vigil. The concern was that when the chapel was built, there were no stairs provided for the choir members to get to the choir loft. A mysterious man showed up at the end of a nine-day prayer vigil and built a spiral staircase. No one knew where he came from, where he purchased his tools, or how he actually built the staircase. It has two complete 360-degree turns, according to Wikipedia and the brochures that are provided at the chapel.

Walking through the door of the chapel after giving the attendant a donation, he gave Mia and Corey an entirely new perspective of what it means to feel God's presence. Neither of them had shared the experience that they had encountered on Christmas night. Corey heard an audible voice expressing words of comfort in the first instance, and he received instructions about the Messiah the second time.

Mia had felt the hand of the Lord touch her on her shoulder. She had never spoken of it.

Now they converged through the doors of the chapel, and they both feel a peace, a warmth, chills.

Corey turned to Mia as they both looked at the staircase in awe, concluding that this had to have been a miracle and what they had both experienced only a few short hours before was also nothing short of miraculous.

They sat on one of the pews while listening to a recording of the history of the staircase. Mia wept and reflected upon her experience during the blizzard when she heard a message on the Internet from a local ministry in Taos. She thought of when she prayed to God for help in knowing him. She thought of Christmas night when she was changed after making a terrible mistake. She continued to weep.

Corey wasn't sure as to whether he should embrace and comfort her or just sit and deal with his own reflections. He chose the latter.

What does it mean to learn of the Messiah? he wondered.

They sat quietly on the pew thinking of what they were experiencing: twenty minutes of silence, twenty minutes of reflection, twenty minutes, twenty minutes of peace.

"This experience was life-changing," spoke Corey, breaking the silence. "Shall we?" He motioned to Mia to rise off of the pew and move on to the plaza.

They both looked at the staircase once more before exiting.

Snow had begun to fall a little heavier now but seemed to be melting quickly. The winds had subsided a bit, but the chill from the cold was prevalent as they opened the doors to the streets. Corey still hadn't shared with Mia about his immediate plans to depart after taking her back to Taos.

They walked until they reached the plaza. Mia noticed several Natives sitting in an area adjacent to the park. She spoke to Corey with an interest to go over to the area. They visited the Palace of the Governors where several Natives display their jewelry.

Mia was interested in getting a sterling silver bracelet. Living in Artesia, New Mexico, did not afford her much opportunities like this. She was ecstatic. There were so many choices. Corey offered to purchase whatever she wanted, but she gestured, "No, I am fine, Corey."

He insisted.

"All right," she relented. "Thank you."

Mia had struggled for many years with receiving from others. She just didn't want to feel obligated to anyone, but now she must learn to give and receive. She selected a lovely sterling silver bracelet, and Corey purchased it from the vendor from Acoma, New Mexico, who was happy to fill the order. The vendor seated next to her had really nice turquoise earrings.

"Just what I have been looking for!" Mia exclaimed with excitement when she saw a pair she really loved. She needed a longer strand with a bulkier style due to her long hair which often fell over her face. She didn't like wearing it in a bun so much. "These would be perfect!"

Corey took it and paid for it as well. "That is all I want for now," she said to Corey.

As they stepped away from the jewelry market, they noticed several people gathered at the center of the park area, seemingly setting up instruments and podiums. Corey boldly stepped over to a gentleman who was standing close by.

"Excuse me, sir. What is the event that seems to be about to take place here?"

"Oh, yes. Messianic groups come out from time to time and share with crowds that gather with singing, dancing, and teaching. They should be getting started shortly."

"Pardon me," said Corey. "I am Corey Hartman, and this is my fiancée, Mia Yazzie."

"My pleasure," responded the gentleman.

"I am Trent. Welcome. You guys are touring today?"

"Yes," said Corey. "And what is a Messianic group?" Trent shared that they are members and leaders of Messianic congregations who come out to evangelize.

Corey hesitantly inquired, "Messianic, meaning?" Somehow, he wanted to understand everything about what Trent spoke.

"So sorry," Trent apologetically said. "This simply means that they are Jewish believers who have accepted Yeshua as Messiah."

Corey was taken aback. *There is that mention of the Messiah again! I cannot believe what is happening to me today!* He became flushed.

"Are you okay, Corey? You look pale," Mia asked with concern in her voice.

Corey turned and looked Mia squarely in her eyes. He *had* to tell her, right there and then!

"I never shared this with you, Mia, but I heard an audible voice two days ago…twice. The first time was when you fainted."

Trent was listening intently.

"The other—"

Mia interrupted, "What did you hear?" but then realized that he was already having a hard time sharing his experience, so she should not cut in. She apologized.

"Sorry, Corey…continue."

"I heard the voice say everything would be okay. And the next time I heard, well, the essence of the message was to follow the Messiah and learn of Him."

This was a lot to take in—so rich, so phenomenal.

They all stood gazing for a while, all trying to process what Corey just said.

Well, here you are Corey. It now begins.

The silence was beginning to be deafening, and Corey changed the subject, "Are you from around here?"

"Yes," Trent responded. "I own a family store on the plaza." He gave them both a card.

"Awesome," said Corey. "Your accent sounds European. Where is home?"

"Frankfurt," Trent replied.

"Then we are brothers," chimed in Corey. "My home is Germany." They shook hands vigorously and laughed.

Corey also gave Trent a card, and they promised to keep in touch with each other. Corey felt the meeting was not by chance but was somehow divinely orchestrated by perhaps the One whose voice he had heard? Perhaps.

Corey appreciated Trent for taking the time to talk with him and answer his questions. "Thank you, my brother," said Corey.

"Thank you as well," Mia spoke up for the first time in a long while.

Trent encouraged them to sit on one of the park benches to enjoy the presentation. He also pointed to the vendors who were selling hot dogs and tamales. Trent strongly suggested that they try the tamales. Mia loved tamales and wanted to taste the Santa Fe version.

Trent left to return to his store.

"Praise Adonai!" were the opening words of the first song riding upon the airwaves from the speakers situated nearby. Corey and Mia hurriedly sat on the park bench to take it all in, at least for as long as possible.

Corey somehow knew that he was to remain for the presentation but would need to leave by three o'clock. He looked at his watch and felt a sense of urgency. Corey still hadn't told Mia he was leaving for Colorado Springs tonight! He settled himself and focused his attention on what was taking place on the makeshift stage.

They stayed for about an hour. Mia found herself caught up in her own world, absolutely exhilarated by the dances, songs, dramas. It felt like an oasis for her thirsty soul. It also drew Corey in. The music, yes, but there was something more.

While enjoying the delightful harmonies and captivating music, Corey eyed someone walking away from the group and coming directly over to him. It seemed as though he had picked Corey right out of the crowd to engage in conversation. The stranger introduced himself to Corey, and from what he said, he learned that the group was from Adat Yeshua. But Corey suspected that the introduction was a build-up for something more—let's say, sacred, more heavenly. It had the ambiance of something holy and did not appear to be random at all. Remembering the two divine visitations he had over the past few days, he now believed that *anything* was possible. His heart shivered with anticipation and not with the cold. Corey listened intently as the member of the group continued to share information about the team, and then, there it was, he mentioned *the Messiah!* This was it! This was what Corey had been waiting for. He stopped the person midsentence and, getting his full attention, with tears in his eyes, Corey asked softly, "Can you tell me about Him? About the *Messiah*?" He did. Corey believed! A warm feeling enveloped his soul. What he was experiencing in his heart was real and could not be denied.

Corey *knew* that his destiny was beginning at that very moment.

He made up his mind that the next important task would be to find a congregation in Colorado Springs to learn and follow the Messiah.

Mia is going to be disappointed, thought Corey.

*****

So much was packed into that one hour. Life-changing things. But they had to go. *We need to head back to Taos,* Corey thought, alarmed that the time had passed so quickly. But no matter how much he wanted to, staying overnight was not going to be a good idea.

He struggled with the decision.

There were too many conflicts: weather issues, company issues. The office had started calling him earlier in the day, and he needed to return to deal with some major client matters.

I would bring Mia back here for our honeymoon, Corey thought, making a mental note. But he must head back to Taos as soon as possible.

CHAPTER 5

BITTERSWEET DEPARTURE

Corey began to rush away from the park. Mia didn't mention the tamales again because his entire attitude had changed; she was not sure what the matter was. They hustled to the vehicle that was parked a short distance away just in time. A mixture of rain and snow had begun to fall.

From the driver's seat Corey mumbled something that sounded like, "Ten after three." He was looking at his watch.

They buckled up and drove through the narrow winding streets of Santa Fe to reach the main highway.

Corey had read several brochures and checked the Internet regarding what is known as "the High Road to Taos."

Mia was concerned. *Seriously? Is Corey seriously thinking of going off the beaten path in this weather? Certainly not!* she concluded before she could ask him. *That would not be a good idea…at all!*

Corey was listening to his GPS to get directions. *Why, there would be no way that we could enjoy the unusual scen-*

ery that is supposed to be along this road if we were to go that route, she argued in her thoughts. She broke the silence.

"Corey, what are you doing?" Her tone was a bit elevated; her anxiety could not be hidden.

"Are you planning to take the High Road to Taos?"

"Yes," he answered, surprised at the fear he heard in her voice. "Is it that you don't trust me? We will be fine."

Mia spoke up. "It is not about trust right now, Corey. It is about wisdom."

"Don't worry so much, Stands With Arms Open. I can handle this. I believe it is only about fifty-six miles when we go this way," said Corey. "Depending on the route, it could take a little longer."

"Yes, but the roads are slippery, and the mountains are no joke!"

After further discussion, Corey still took the High Road to Taos.

Mia was livid. She pulled her clothes close to her bosom, pulled an afghan out of her bag, covered herself, then turned toward the door of the vehicle.

The roads were not good, but then Corey knew this. What he was actually dealing with, she had no idea, however, it did appear that he was to meet an appointment. It was all so strange. They were, for miles, the only vehicle on the road.

Mia felt nervous and terribly concerned. She tried to sleep, but sleep escaped her. She tried to locate music on the radio, but the frequency was poor.

She whispered a prayer.

"God, be with us. Please help us to get back to Taos safely. And help me to understand what Corey is dealing with. Amen."

After several hours of touch and go, up the mountain, down the mountain, dipping roads, and silence—strong silence that spoke louder than words—they reached the street where she was lodging. What normally would have taken them about an hour, took over two hours—much longer than what Corey anticipated—but Mia was grateful.

"Thank you, God. Thank you!"

Corey turned off the ignition with a push of a button then reached over to Mia, who by now had removed her afghan and was sitting up, alert.

He slightly pinched her chin as in a gesture to cheer her up, then he dropped his head and released a very heavy sigh. He reached over to open her door, and Mia grabbed his arm, though gently, and asked, "Corey, what is going on with you?" He did not answer.

He got out of the SUV and leaned against the door as if in much distress. Mia could not take the suspense and jumped out of the vehicle as Corey said, "No, I am coming around to you." She was headed to his side of the car.

"Look, Mia, I have to leave in a few minutes to depart for Colorado—"

She did not allow him to finish what he was saying. "You what?" exclaimed Mia. "What on earth is going on with you? You rush us back to Taos in crazy weather, you don't say a word to me all day, nor yesterday, about return-ing to Colorado, then you shove this news flash before me as though I was a stranger, then you expect me to just accept it? I deserve much, much more from you than this. How dare you tell me on your way out that you are leaving in a few minutes? Is something wrong with you? And to top it off, all weather reports are pointing to stay at home, do not brave the storm, and you want to travel? How are you getting to Colorado Springs? Flying? Tell me!"

Corey was struggling with how to deal with his new-found experience with his Messiah. He doesn't know what his life is supposed to be like now and how his relationship with Mia fits into this new way or new place in his life. Confusion was unquestionably overtaking him. It was swallowing him up like the wave of a tsunami. He felt as though he was drowning in uncertainty.

Mia continued berating him. "When you have an issue to confront or any type of conflict, you vanish to sort it out. I don't have that luxury. I face what is bothering me. I deal with confrontation. Is this what I should prepare to look forward to when I become your wife?"

He tried to speak.

At the same time, a guest walked out of the door of their unit and asked, "Is everything okay?"

Corey said, "Yes. All is well."

"All right then," the gentleman said, appearing to be satisfied with Corey's answer. He walked to his car.

This bed-and-breakfast offered individual units, which provided privacy and convenience for guests rather than have everyone enter the same common area to reach their rooms. The common area was set up only for socializing and meals.

The guest who was concerned about them simply cranked up his car to let it run a bit, then headed back inside. He advised, "Not a good night to be on the roads."

"Thanks," replied Corey.

Mia looked at him with fire in her eyes and said, "You know what? You can just do what you want to do, but I can't and will not do this with you!" She turned and went up the slippery steps carefully, saying, "I am getting out of this freezing weather."

She went inside hoping that he would come in as well to console her and let her know that he was sorry and that he would wait a day or so before traveling. He didn't.

Instead, Corey went to his SUV rental, called Enterprise just before they closed at seven to have them pick up the vehicle, located an Uber driver, and left abruptly. He didn't look back.

Mia was heartbroken as she looked out of the window and watched him leave as the car disappeared in the distance.

She decided to turn on the television to see what the weather predictions were looking like, as though it would change Corey's mind. At this point, she tried to fight back the tears and negative thoughts of where the engagement would be headed at this point.

The phone rang. It was Corey. The still upset Mia let it go to voicemail. She was hurting too deeply to talk with him.

"Leave a message with your name, date, and time that you called, and I will return your call as soon as possible," the recording on Mia's phone instructed in a businesslike tone.

Corey's voice came through loud and clear. "I love you so much, Mia. Please give me a day to sort things out. I don't know what it means to follow the Messiah or learn of

Him. I don't know what I'm supposed to do to make that happen. I know I have hurt you, but just trust me, I will speak with you and see you soon."

She listened intently to the voicemail, not knowing what to make of it. At the sound of his voice, she broke down in tears. After a while, to try and calm herself, Mia decided to make a cup of tea and sit in her favorite spot, but the tears would not *stop*! On the way to the kitchen, she made a detour to retrieve a box of tissue from the bath area and made a futile effort to sap up the evidence of her broken heart. She looked at herself in the bathroom mirror. Her eyes were puffy and red. "Lord, make it stop! The pain! The tears!"

After a few minutes, she got some relief.

Calming down quite a bit, Mia started to mull Corey's message over and over in her mind. The more she reflected on what he said, the more she somehow felt that everything would work out between the two of them, though their relationship was severely fractured at the moment—*severely*.

She had recovered enough to make another attempt to go to the kitchen to try to make her tea without breaking down again. She chose a peppermint-flavored tea as she boiled the water in a beautiful red-and-silver tea kettle. Looking at the clock, it was almost eight o'clock. Mia made her tea and went to sit in the living area by the fireplace. She pulled the blanket over her lap that was hanging over the chair and surfed the channels on the TV set for the weather report. "Snow, snow, and more snow," said the meteorologist, "mixed with freezing rain. Stay home unless you absolutely must be out."

"Oh well," whispered Mia, while realizing all of a sudden how hungry she was. She and Corey were supposed to go for sushi in Santa Fe in the early afternoon. She was truly looking forward to ordering a delectable shrimp or salmon tempura roll with wasabi.

Corey had promised to take her but instead rushed back to Taos and then dropped a bombshell about returning to Colorado Springs right away. She also remembered the tamales she didn't get. Now she was even more disappointed. Santa Fe was about shopping and enjoying world-renowned restaurants where chefs from around the world came and joined the famous Santa Fe cultures. She missed out on doing the latter.

Mia searched for something to eat. She couldn't believe that there was only a box of saltines, a can of tuna, and a banana in the kitchen. Her improvised meal was not very appetizing, but it was better than just having, maybe, water and tea.

The pain of the experience was still lingering, pressing against Mia's heart.

Perhaps if Corey can locate a Messianic congregation in Colorado Springs, the experience would help him "sort things out" as he claimed. She too thought of sorting things out regarding her faith. Perhaps it was time to read some Bible verses or listen to a Bible teacher. She went to her bedroom to get her laptop that she normally travelled with, brought it into the living area, and went on to YouTube.

Where do you begin with this? she wondered.

An ad for a television series called *The Chosen* popped up.

"*The Chosen*?" she asked silently. "That is certainly *not* me!"

However, the title intrigued her, and she clicked on it. The sound of the music and the appearance of the characters sparked her interest even further. She decided to watch as much of the ad as possible. She learned that *The Chosen* is a television drama based on the life of Jesus Christ. The series portrays Jesus through the eyes of those who met him.

The captivating ad was only the beginning. Mia knew that she had to set up the app to view the show in its entirety.

Episode after episode of *The Chosen* passed across Mia's computer screen. It was an incredible series.

What allured her the most was the great magnitude of love the Christ evidently has for tainted and hurting humanity. "I certainly fall into those categories," Mia contemplated, "especially after what I did with Corey." But strangely enough, she felt her guilt-ridden heart being washed by the loving mercies of the Son of God—Jesus the Christ. She longed to know Him more. Her life was being transformed with every moment that she watched the show.

Mia knew that embarking upon this series was no accident, but rather God's hand guiding her. She whispered a prayer, "God, I am thankful."

Mia was finally able to drag herself away from what felt like a holy habitation. She needed to get to bed, as it had been a long, tiresome day. She thought of Corey and tried not to burst into a crying fit again.

She went to the kitchen and disposed of the banana peel in the trash, washed her cup, then turned off the light in the living room area. It was time for bed!

Before retiring, she took a hot shower, climbed into some comfy satin pajamas, wrapped her hair neatly in a spiral hornlike shape with a scarf, and then got under the warm cozy covers. Her head could not have hit the pillow soon enough.

She immediately drifted off into a deep sleep around twelve midnight and slept well into the morning. When she awoke, the pain and discomfort that she had felt in her chest the previous night was no longer there. She felt better today. Lighter. More hopeful.

She slipped out of bed into her white feather-and-satin slippers and went to the window, pulled back the curtains, and saw snow everywhere.

"This is Taos in the winter," Mia said to herself, laughing for the first time in hours! The sight of the dazzling white snow sparkling as the sunshine hit it from different angles was picture-perfect! This was a dream while it lasted, but the experience was swiftly coming to an end. She was scheduled to go back to Artesia, New Mexico, today after a great three-week vacation, but now it looked as if she would be staying over an extra day or two due to the weather.

Her mind started to shift back into work mode. There were so many projects that needed her attention back at the office. She needed to leave, but today was impossible. She learned that Highway-68 and I-25 had not been cleared. The city workers were limited. The newscasters were explicit. "The roads are dangerous, and many airports have closed."

Airports?

The mention of the word *airports* catapulted Mia's thoughts right back to Corey and the fiasco that she had experienced with him the previous night. *Airports? Where was Corey? What on—*

A knock at the door pulled her away from her worry for the moment. Another knock. She scurried to the door.

"Good morning, Ms. Stands With Arms Open. Well, may I come in? I have your breakfast here."

Disoriented, Mia quickly welcomed Mrs. Garcia in and motioned for her to place the breakfast on the table, as usual.

"Hola¡ Como estas?" she asked Mia.

"Just a bit tired, but I am okay, thank you very much. If the roads are clear enough to pass tomorrow, I will depart early, so no breakfast please. Thank you so much for your splendid hospitality. I have so enjoyed your place."

Mia was tired of speaking with Mrs. Garcia, who kept standing as though she had a concern.

"So you sure everything is okay, eh?"

"Yes, yes!" Mia responded.

"Sorry to see you go. Please come again, will you?"

"Certainly," replied Mia, moving toward the door as a *hopefully* subtle gesture to say, "Please go now." She hoped Ms. Garcia got the *unspoken* message. Mia did not mean to be rude, but she was *really* not in the mood for company.

Mia felt a sudden sadness but quickly shook it off. It had been a great experience being at The Place B&B most of the month of December. The year 2017 had been so special for her. She was living a dream that she had for years, in spite of the tree incident and Corey's outrageous behavior of travelling in questionable weather.

She looked forward to a new year with endless possibilities. The oil industry was doing relatively well, and her position at the company was great—*challenging* but great.

She sat at the dining table to eat a scrumptious breakfast at the bed-and-breakfast. At home in Artesia, it was mostly bagels and sour cream, or toast and hot chocolate. Always on the run.

Her cell phone rang. It was Corey. "Mia, please talk with me. I apologize again." He sounded despairing.

She responded with "Good morning, Corey. How did you find Colorado Springs upon your arrival?" She was being sarcastic.

"Mia, I am at Taos Regional Airport Hotel. The airport closed last night, and it looks as though I'll be stuck here another day."

"Sorry about your plight, Corey. Can we talk later?"
Silence.

"All right, Mia," Corey spoke hesitantly. "I will call you later."

He hung up and she began to think of how hurt she had been last night and honestly even at the present moment. She needed a little more time before discussing anything with Corey.

"My breakfast! By now it is cold!" She ate the blueberry muffin and a small spoon of fruit salad, sipped some hot chocolate, and went to her bedroom.

Since I would be going nowhere today, this seems to be a good time to catch up on some lost sleep, Mia thought. She got into bed and dozed off after about fifteen minutes.

She slept until noon and awoke feeling famished. There was no food in her refrigerator nor cabinets except crackers. She missed Corey. He would have thought of something.

"Oh, there is a bakery across the street." She checked. It was closed.

She called Mrs. Garcia. "I know you do not provide lunch, but I have no food here and the roads are still dangerous. Could I bother you for a bite to eat? I feel really bad about this."

Mrs. Garcia pleasantly replied, "Not a bother at all. I happen to have some ham and cheese here. I can make a sandwich and add a bowl of chicken soup. I'll send it by my niece who is here for a visit. Enjoy, Mia. When you leave tomorrow just leave the key on the kitchen counter. Safe travels. See you next time."

CHAPTER 6

RETURN TO ARTESIA

Hearing Mrs. Garcia's repeated farewells prompted Mia to consider packing for her departure. She had put packing off for too long but realized it must be done. Hopefully, the roads will be clear enough to travel. She sighed softly as she thought of Corey.

"So many beautiful memories of this place, but I really need to get on the road tomorrow." She sighed again. "What if the city workers have not been able to get much done? Ugh! This is frustrating." She beat the air with her fists.

Thinking intensely, Mia wished that they could have overnighted at Santa Fe. *I wanted to experience staying in a hacienda.* She was uncertain whether she would get another chance to visit or not. Corey did not say when and if they would return. She was unaware that he had pondered the idea.

By morning Mia began to retrieve her belongings from the dresser drawers on the closet. The tears returned.

"Why am I crying again?" she questioned. "Enough already!

"My heart aches, and tomorrow I leave this beautiful place—Taos—with its scenic city and galleries to die for, quaint shops, eating places, adobes, mountains. On bright sunny days, it was a haven for artists from all over the world," she reflected. Mia hadn't decided what time she might begin her more-than-five-hour drive to Artesia. She just knew that it was past time to go. E-mails were overflowing; text messages were taking over her phone. She was not yet in the mood for returning to the office, but as Vice President of Choice Wells, it was her responsibility to make sure that no harm come to the local residents due to the crude oil production at the refineries. These issues could become political and controversial very quickly. The situation would require that she remained focused at all times. This was her main concern as she packed. How do you focus in the midst of emotional pain from disappointments and unrealized expectations? Perhaps she would consider transferring to another Choice Wells company that wasn't having so many issues at the moment.

Leaving the company wasn't really an option. Mia had done very well during her eight years there. She was quick on her feet, sharp in appearance and demeanor, proficient and efficient—a model executive. Mia Stands With Arms Open concluded, after much thought, "I will return with tenacity and determination to get through this situation with Corey."

He called again. "Mia, can we please talk for a moment?" he asked.

"Go ahead, Corey. I am listening," she said.

Corey proceeded. "I did not want to hurt you, dear."

Mia smirked.

"Sorry, Corey. That was wrong of me," she quickly apologized. "Please continue."

"I was excited about our trip to Santa Fe and was so looking forward to staying over, as I said in our own rooms, of course."

Mia chimed in, "Of course!"

He continued hoping not to be interrupted again with Mia's sarcasm.

"I was just so overwhelmed with our experience at the plaza until I felt like just running away from what I was feeling, especially the things that I didn't understand. I know that running or shutting down is not the answer to problem solving. I grew up with much better values than that. But, as you know, I had never—until Christmas Day—experienced hearing a mysterious audible voice speak to me. To top it off, one of the messages from the voice indicated that I should learn of Messiah. Look what happened at the plaza. There were people there who were lecturing and singing about Messiah. That could not have been a coincidence, Mia. But I don't know how to process this, and I don't want to lose you. Please try to understand that my rash behavior was not healthy for either of us, and it will not happen again. Will you accept my deepest apology?"

Mia paused then replied, "Yes, Corey. I accept your apology. Are you asking for forgiveness?"

"I suppose that is what I am doing. Please forgive me."

"I forgive you, Corey…I forgive you," Mia softened a bit. Continuing, Mia said, "I think you should contact Trent or the guy that you spoke with from the Messianic congregation. I am sure he would be delighted to help you sort things out.

"Do you have his card, Corey?" she inquired. He replied in the affirmative. "Then call him after we hang up. As for the voices you heard, it was more than likely God's voice in some way calling you to serve Him. I am brand-new at this, but I have been reading some Bible verses on my PC and watching an incredible series about the life of Jesus. My life is changing by the moment. I will send you the link. Watch it. It will transform you as well." She changed the tone of the dialogue. "Where are you, Corey?"

"I am at the hotel by the airport preparing to get my overnight luggage downstairs and check out. The airport has opened. My flight is slightly delayed, but I will be able to fly out in under three hours' time. I suppose I should have flown my jet…just an afterthought."

"All right, Corey," she said after a long sigh. "Have a safe trip. I am finishing my packing so that I can get on the road by nine this morning. There is so much to be done before the thirty-first, which is actually the end of our fiscal year."

Corey asked with hesitation, "Are we okay now, Mia?"

"I am still wearing my engagement ring, but I am not very clear as to where we are at the moment as an engaged couple, Corey," she emphatically declared. "I will contact you in a few days, but definitely before New Year's Eve."

Corey was disappointed.

"I will call you," Mia said again. The calls were disconnected. They both felt an emptiness as the connection was not what either of them had hoped for. Things were left hanging.

While Mia finished up packing, Corey pulled out the card of the representative from the Messianic congregation. He took a long hard look at it before making a move.

His name was Aaron. "Okay. I will call."

"Hello, Aaron here."

"Aaron, this is Corey Hartman. We met at the plaza in Santa Fe a few days ago?" Corey hoped he remembered him.

"Of course!" responded Aaron. "I remember you and a lady with you. Do you live in New Mexico?" he asked.

"I am from Colorado, but my fiancée is living in Artesia, New Mexico."

The conversation briefly continued between the two of them as they reconnected.

*****

In the meantime, Mia started heading out to her car with her luggage and personal hand items. She took an overall look back at her beloved bed-and-breakfast, which had felt so much like a new home over the past few weeks. The suite was second to none with a spacious living area, dining area, kitchen breakfast nook—which was nearly destroyed by the fallen outdoor Christmas tree—spacious bedroom and bath, plus a great powder room. It was color-fully decorated with beautiful New Mexico paintings, rugs, and furniture throughout.

She looked around each room for the third time, finally determining it was time to go. "Perhaps next year I will return, or maybe I would spend a few days at Red River,

New Mexico, another one of the most beautiful places in the States."

Mia left the key on the kitchen counter as Mrs. Garcia had instructed, pulled the door close, and slowly walked down the steps. Her fur boots were the best choice for travel today. She would remove her faux leather knee-length coat upon getting into her rental car. She had booked it as a round trip from Artesia. At the moment, this didn't seem to have been the brightest idea. Nevertheless, it was all going to work out after staying over the agreed number of days.

It was very cool that morning, even with the additional protection of a red scarf, gloves, and a fur cap. Mia cleaned as much snow off the car as possible until the resident neighbor from the previous night offered to help with the rest. He convinced her that he had everything needed to scrape and blow the snow.

"Thanks," Mia shouted to him as he returned to his unit.

"Hope everything works out for you and the fellow." She supposed he was referring to Corey. They had argued, and the neighbor was concerned. He appeared to have a slight defect as he walked away, waving his hand without looking back.

Hungry, Mia turned on the ignition, even though she noticed that the bakery was open. "I had better go and perhaps get something along the way," she said, wondering how that may work out, knowing that it would be a fairly long drive—too long of a drive to keep on her coat, gloves, cap, and scarf.

Mia struggled to shed the items and place them in the back seat. She sat for a brief moment, gave out a sigh, and looked at the radio as if to determine what radio station to listen to on the road. She began to serve the FM stations, running across a song that spoke of the love of Jesus.

"Perfect!" she said, clapping her hands briefly. The music sounded great, though she wasn't sure how long the frequency would be strong enough to enjoy the music. Mia drove off and headed toward the main highway, enjoying the Christian music. The roads were not so bad. She was grateful.

After driving for about three hours, Mia began to look for signs indicating a rest stop providing food. I-25 constitutes pueblos every ten to fifteen miles. She looked for signs advertising fry bread. After about another forty-five minutes she decided to stop at one of the casinos. They always had food and hopefully the fry bread she was yearning for. Mia chanced it at Buffalo Thunder. She went in to check for it and was disappointed. Later she tried Sandia Pueblo. At last! There was a full buffet which *did* display fry bread, a Native American bread made from flour and with a touch of baking powder, hot water, and deep-fried in very hot oil. This was just the right place to stop. The buffet had several stations: pizza, Asian fusion, native dishes, sandwiches, whatever you may have had a taste for, it was on the buffet.

Mia prepared a plate and sat at a table for two, though it was only her dining. She didn't want to select a table for three or four. The food was delicious. After taking care of personal needs, Mia resumed her trip. Her thoughts were now directed toward home and Choice Wells. She began to look forward to returning to her condo. She had lived in her place for about four years now. She loved the open concept layout that New Mexico developers are so famous for, and the lighting, that's key. Her decorator, who she had met at a home show, captured her attention. He got the job and decorated her place with exquisite taste and design. Mia loved the new color combination of grays and reds and the inclusion of beautiful native-designed area rugs.

The last two or more hours passed swiftly, as the radio continued to release one beautiful song after another. The "Hallelujahs" and "Praise Him" just touched Mia so much until she felt encouraged when she saw the signs for Artesia and finally turned into her street. It was a small town of about 11,000 people but a town with great ambitions, boasting of three oil refineries. However, along with that comes more often than not, some chemical issues, and that's where she steps into the scenario as a chemical engineer. It was challenging, but it kept her motivated with her work.

This is home to crude oil—Artesia, New Mexico.

Mia turned the key to her condo and was surprised with a beautiful bouquet of flowers.

Where? Who? The questions zipped through her mind. She dropped her handbag and some items that were in her hands and rushed to see who had sent such a beautiful display of orchids and other types of flowers. Her housekeeper had gone to her home the day before she left Taos to refresh the house, shop for groceries, to make sure that all of her favorite foods were in the cabinets and fridge, but she would not have sent flowers, *would she?*

Opening the card, her suspicions were confirmed. They were from Corey.

"Enjoy your flowers. Enjoy being home. Much love, Corey," the message read.

How thoughtful and how lovely, she thought. Locating her cell phone, she called him. He answered immediately.

"Mia, it is so good to hear your voice," he said with enthusiasm. "You are home," he gleefully continued.

"Yes, Corey. I am home, and I love the bouquet. Thank you so much. And I *do* miss you. I must tell you I do."

"Mia, I want so much to be there with you, but I am so far behind with my work—"

She stopped him. "Corey, no, you don't have to apologize. I am okay. Yes, I was very hurt, and I am yet working through some things, but I am much better now. We both have a lot of work to do with our jobs. I don't know how it is going to all come together."

She sat on her beautiful gray loveseat to finish her conversation.

Corey began speaking about having connected with Aaron and how he had some plans to attend a special fellowship meeting at one of the Jewish Messianic communities by Friday.

Mia's thoughts went directly to her office. She made a mental note to call upon hanging up with Corey.

"Corey," Mia interrupted, "I think that is a great idea. Be sure and let me know how it goes. I literally just walked into the house, so please allow me to call you back after I get settled."

"All right, Mia. Sure." Corey wondered if he had turned her off with the religious content of his conversation. Corey was extremely excited because he was venturing into new but necessary territory if his life was going to make a difference as a man and as Mia's future husband. He looked forward to the fellowship that was coming up on Friday evening with trepidation and excitement all at the same time. These feelings were strange for him.

Mia called her executive assistant, Anna.

"Mia, where are you?" asked Anna.

"I am back…just got in. Anna, look, I need to get settled here before I come in. You haven't set any appointments for today, have you? Please don't tell me you have," Mia pleaded.

"No, but Mr. Eckridge has been e-mailing and calling over and over again. He needs to meet with you desperately to go over some community issues."

"Anna, not today please. Perhaps day after tomorrow."

Mia began to feel fatigued from the long drive from Taos. Rest was the best next thing for her to do so that she could have a clear head tomorrow.

The doorbell rang, followed by a key turning. It was Hadash, her housekeeper, cook, personal assistant. Hadash was that and more.

"Mia!" she screamed with excitement. "So, so happy you are back! How we have all missed you."

Mia replied, somewhat unsmilingly, "I've missed you too, but, Hadash, you *did* see my car in the garage with the door opened, right?"

Hadash nodded. "Yes."

"So you should have waited for me to answer, true?"

"Yes, you are right. So sorry," she said with embarrassment. A traditional way in some African cultures is for the younger women to be addressed as "Auntie" and for the older women to be addressed as "Ma." Hadash remembered her manners.

Hadash was a Sudanese immigrant from Northeast Africa, whose parents had lived for many years in Europe until they finally gained all the papers necessary to move to the U.S. and eventually attain citizenship. Hadash's parents became situated in New York. Hadash had visited a long-time family friend a few years prior in El Paso and learned of job opportunities in Artesia. She decided to make the move from New York. Mia had met her through a coworker, and she just seemed to be a good fit.

Hadash immediately began to get Mia's belongings from the car and picked up items that she had dropped earlier. She had been the one to receive the flower delivery and, of course, replenish the kitchen with the necessary food and staples. Mia always provided a budget for such things so that Hadash could manage the condo properly.

Finally settling in a bit, Mia decided that a hot shower and some rest would be ideal for the moment. She asked Hadash to prepare a nice tossed salad and baked salmon for dinner.

"Anything else, Auntie?"

"Yes, of course. Boiled white potatoes."

"Yes, Auntie. At what time?"

"Around six thirty this evening,"

Acknowledgment of the instructions was followed by a quick bow by Hadash, which is another aspect of the African culture which is done as they speak. The bow is more of a courtesy gesture and one of affirmation.

When Mia was first addressed this way, she quickly stopped Hadash, concerned that she was out of place for doing it, but checking around a bit with colleagues, she realized that bowing was a custom which showed high respect. This gesture is extended by the women, as the men bend over toward the person that they are addressing, using the expression "Ma" or "Auntie" for females or "Daddy" and "Papa" for males, depending on the age of the person being addressed.

Hadash went directly to the kitchen to sort out the remaining items from grocery shopping and to begin prepping for dinner. It was already four twenty in the afternoon.

Mia went to her bedroom and crawled into her freshly made-up bed of lavender eight-hundred-thread sheets, a pillow top mattress cover over a Beauty Rest firm mattress.

"Finally," she said, pulling the sheets and comforter slightly over her head. The house was cozy and, yes, there was a fireplace in her very spacious bedroom. Sleep was welcomed. She dreamed of Corey and their wedding.

As a child Mia dreamed often, quickly telling Grannie Yazzie about her dreams. Grannie would say, "Your visions are talking of things to come, Mia. Be careful who you speak to about what you see in dreams. The Great One speaks to you."

Mia wasn't sure of whom she referred to then as the Great One, but looking back now, Grannie Yazzie was probably referring to God as she knew Him and would be the same God whom she serves now and loves as her Lord.

The dream confirmed to Mia that she and Corey would one day marry. She awakened about an hour and a half later to a pleasant and wonderful aroma coming from the kitchen. Hadash always knew how to prepare food with the best of herbs and seasonings. She realized that Mia didn't mention bread, but Hadash knew how to prepare fry bread, thanks to Mia's tutelage. And there it was, in the midst of the spread before her, what she had been hankering for all throughout her long drive back from Taos.

"Ah! Fry bread," whispered Mia. Dinner will be so special.

She now thought of Corey again, who had been so excited earlier when she spoke with him about attending the Messianic congregation on Friday, which was going to be tomorrow. She spoke aloud, "Tomorrow!" *I should call Corey.*

Corey answered the phone after only one ring.

"Stands With Arms Open! Finally, I get to speak with you."

"Corey, we spoke earlier."

"I know, my dear, but I want to speak with you often, even on the same day," he said with sincerity.

"I wanted to say," Mia quickly responded, "that I am excited for you that you will have a chance to visit the Messianic congregation tomorrow evening. Perhaps you will meet some really neat people and get some of your questions answered." She spoke confidently.

"Thanks for the vote of confidence," replied Corey.

"I was thinking of you"—she didn't want to mention her dream—"and just, well, I wanted to just let you know that I am happy for you. My dinner will be on the table soon, Corey. Good evening." She disconnected quickly. Corey wondered why she was being so abrupt.

Dinner was simply amazing; all credits went to Hadash. Hadash was a live-in housekeeper and personal assistant. On her days off, she would go to El Paso to visit family and friends, but she didn't take off too much because she felt as though Mia really needed her help. Even on designated days off or when Mia traveled out, she stayed at Mia's home, keeping busy.

Mia came to the conclusion that Hadash didn't *really* want to visit family for whatever reason. She made sure that Hadash knew that she was at home in Artesia and that it was okay if she didn't want to travel out.

CHAPTER 7

THE OFFICE

Mia began to focus that evening on her duties at the office. Tomorrow would be busy. Board meetings and briefings about some community issues that were brewing. Time to rest.

Mia awakened around six in the morning and went for a brisk walk since the weather was favorable. After which, she made preparations to go to the office. Passing on breakfast, she thought of grabbing bagels with cream cheese and coffee once she arrived at her workplace.

Before going into her office, Mia went directly to the break room for the anticipated bagels and coffee. The executive director of their company was seated at one of the tables drinking coffee and enjoying a donut.

"Morning, Mia," he said. "Welcome back."

She responded with "Good morning, Les."

Les was always energetic and excited about anything happening at the office that he could become privy to: weddings, pregnancies, breakups, or anything else that engendered gossip.

"So how was your leave time, Mia?" he inquired.

Mia didn't feel up to sharing anything with him.

"Fine, Les," she answered guardedly and left the break-room in a hurry.

The boardroom was full of employees emitting a low buzz of chatter.

"Welcome back, Mia," each one said.

"Thanks," she responded.

Enough of the frivolities for her sake. There was *work* to be done.

A presentation from Marketing was pitched, and they were all briefed on community issues regarding pollution complaints on the horizon about their refineries. Mia took extensive notes, determined that she would not get involved in any heated discussions on her first day back. She kept a low profile and was happy when the two-hour meeting was over. Anna came in to alert her that she had an appointment with two mentees from New Mexico State University in Carlsbad at two in the afternoon and that she must meet with Mr. Eckridge on Monday at ten thirty in the morning.

She threw her head back and emphatically said, "Anna! Okay, I will see him." Mr. Eckridge was a community activist who was assigned by the local organizations that were established to keep oil companies accountable. She wasn't sure if it was the urban league or which civil rights organization, nevertheless, Mr. Eckridge was always thorough and insisted on having her review any statistics that would indicate that a potential problem was brewing.

Lunchtime gave her a breather before she got together with the mentees who met with her monthly for their engineering classes. Her role was to show them how an engineer can be a viable businesswoman or man and how engineering has many facets. The mentees were delightful to work with.

Her meeting with them in the afternoon went well. Her agenda for the remainder of the day consisted of two items: a delicious dinner and rest. Saturday was rest day.

The days at the office, moving forward, turned into weeks of meetings with staff, the board, luncheons, and more mentoring. The first of January had found her refreshed and motivated following a great New Year's Eve dinner with friends. By the end of January, Mia had run out of steam. She reflected on a rally that Mr. Eckridge had asked her to support by addressing key issues.

During her meeting with him, he went on and on about how she could be influential in addressing climate change in the community and actually statewide. He wanted Choice Wells to cut back on production by adjusting their hours and days of production. He was adamant about local families beginning to complain about issues with their lungs and showed Mia medical documentation to prove it. She could see in the report that there certainly were some real health issues, but it was going to take a massive investigation to link them to her company.

Mia's first compromise to show that Choice Wells was concerned about the community and interested in doing what was needful to address climate change issues was to agree to speak at an upcoming rally. This she did, not long after she met with Mr. Eckridge. Her message gave the company a temporary break, but it was not going to be enough to stop the complaints from pouring in over the next few months.

Leaving the office for that day, she answered a call from Corey while waving goodbye to Anna who was walking out the door.

What was Anna thinking? Mia wondered. She could hear Anna's voice saying, "Ms. Yazzie still doesn't get it. Relationships need attention. You can't just squeeze in a moment here and a moment there to chat with someone that you say you love and plan to marry." Mia had shared with Anna and a few other friends on New Year's Eve that she was engaged.

"Congrats!" they all said.

"So where is your fiancé?" they asked.

"In Colorado," she answered. The conversation ended on that note.

"Hello, Corey."

"Mia. How are you?" he asked.

"A bit tired but pretty much okay," she continued.

"Should I fly down to spend some time with you this weekend? You know I will bear my own lodging expenses."

"I know, Corey, but, I—" She hesitated. "Why don't we look at a weekend in February? Say, maybe, Valentine's week?"

Corey was a little perplexed, but he moved on with the conversation.

"Sure. So then, when can we find time to discuss our wedding?" He pushed the envelope a bit.

She said, "Well, maybe next weekend…we can FaceTime?"

"Mia, that weekend is Valentine's weekend."

She sounded frustrated when she replied, "Okay, Corey. Let's discuss the plans when you come down to Artesia." There was a sharp tinge to her voice.

Corey looked at his cell phone. *Hmm! What's going on with Mia?* he asked himself. Corey decided to give her some space and purposed to work on some projects for his company over the weekend to keep himself busy. That should keep his mind off things for a while. Something was really going on with Mia, and he could not figure out what it was.

The weekend slipped by pretty quickly, and Mia began to recall her Friday afternoon conversation with Corey.

"Oh no!" she exclaimed, disgusted with herself. "I never asked him how things were going with his visits to the Messianic congregation." She wondered how Corey felt about her seeming lack of interest.

She also purposed in her heart to do something about her own spiritual quest. *I need to find a church to attend. I have no excuse,* she mused.

Preparing to go to the office, she heard Hadash in the kitchen.

"No breakfast again, Mia?" she asked.

"No," answered Mia, running again.

Hadash took the chance and spoke boldly to Mia, "You really ought to see to yourself, Auntie. You look a bit pale. You are not eating properly. Bagels, donuts, and coffee—no good for you day in and day out!"

Mia responded loudly to what she felt was insubordination on Hadash's part, "I don't pay you to tell me what I should or should not do! You are out of line!"

"Sorry, Auntie," the remorseful Hadash quickly retorted with a quick bow. "Sorry."

Mia shut the door behind her and placed her things in the back seat of her car. She thought for a moment that she should not have been so harsh with Hadash. She went back inside and apologized, wondering why she was behaving this way. *Why am I so irritable?* she questioned herself, puzzled. *This is not me.*

When she arrived at the office, she asked Anna to locate some churches in the area that may be good for her to visit. Anna was shocked.

"Excuse me, ma'am? But what—" She struggled to overcome her surprise at Mia's request. "Um…well…any specifics?" Anna eventually inquired after pulling herself together.

"I don't know, Anna. Can you just help me out?"

Anna smiled and said to Mia, "You are welcome at my church."

Mia never thought to ask Anna if she attended a church before this moment. Anna continued, "The praise and worship is exuberant, the dance ministry is beautiful, and my pastor is absolutely a great teacher of the Word of God. Please come on Sunday. I can pick you up at, let's say…nine thirty? Service starts at ten."

"Yes," Mia joyfully answered. "Thanks, Anna."

"Sure."

*****

The service was more than Mia could have imagined. Life-changing. She actually went down to the altar to answer the call for salvation.

Mia Stands With Arms Open officially asked the Lord to come into her heart. What an amazing day and amazing decision.

Now to tell Corey, she thought. *What will he say?*

After three rings she hung up the phone, then decided to dial again. He answered.

"Mia," he asked, "why did you hang up before I answered?"

She didn't know what to say, but she *did* share the good news that she had accepted Jesus as Lord of her life and she wanted him to know. He was excited to hear this because he had made a decision, weeks prior, to accept Jesus as his Messiah. He just didn't tell Mia. He learned at temple, which was where he attended each week, that God had been speaking to him audibly since the first time he supernaturally heard His voice. Now Corey understood that God had a special call on his life as a German Jewish believer.

Mia couldn't be happier for him.

Anna was elated as well about Mia's most important decision in her life. Mia invited Anna to her home to share dinner as they discussed more about her new walk.

Hadash had prepared roast beef with carrots and potatoes over brown rice and fresh green beans on the side.

The afternoon was beautiful. After Anna's visit, Mia spoke again with Corey then retired for the night after going over some figures for Choice Wells. She made a mental note to follow up on a couple of checks written to a company in Oklahoma that seemed questionable.

CHAPTER 8

THE LOSS

Anna was delighted to see a new Mia on Monday. She took a cup of coffee into Mia's office as she went over her schedule. The phone rang, and Anna went to her desk to answer it.

"Les, yes," she said. "One moment." She dialed Mia. "Les is on line 2."

"My dear Mia, pack your bags. You must travel on Friday."

"Travel? Are you serious? Travel where?"

"You are going to Dubai!"

"Dubai? No way, Les! Dubai? Friday? What for?" Of course, Dubai was a place that Mia always dreamed of going; her interest was piqued. "What is this about, Les?"

"We got a call from one of our refineries here in Artesia, telling us that the designated delegate for an international conference being held there next Monday had to cancel, so you are it…the replacement," said Les, with a light sense of humor.

"Seriously, Les?" she said.

"Seriously! We will give Anna the entire itinerary, and she will travel with you."

Mia screamed with excitement, "I can't believe it!" *Okay, calm down, Mia,* she told herself.

Anna also squealed with delight when Les informed her. She even ran around her desk and danced.

The news of the trip to Dubai spread throughout the office like wildfire. In the next ten minutes after hearing the information from Les, Mia looked up from her desk and saw five staff members standing in the doorway and chatting with Anna. They sought to gain entrance, but they knew that they could not break protocol by just walking in, so they anxiously awaited a signal from Stands With Arms Open to please come in. She beckoned them with gestures of welcome.

One of the executive assistants from the second floor spoke up and said, "So we hear you're going to Dubai as a delegate from Choice Wells, Artesia, New Mexico."

"Yes," answered Mia with excitement in her voice. "Yes, yes!" She could not contain herself.

"So tell us when. For how long?" spoke up another staff member.

"Now, Laura, I don't have any details as of yet. At the same time, we cannot be holding this conversation at length, you understand, correct?"

"Of course," Laura replied, "I'd better get back to work."

"Good idea," Mia concurred. The others filed behind the executive assistant and Laura, feeling left out, as they did not get a chance to share their excitement and ask their questions.

Anna entered Mia's office as the group was leaving. "Ms. Yazzie, you are aware that I don't have the itinerary yet, right?" she inquired with a slight hesitancy.

Mia, speaking with a calmer demeanor, said, "I know, Anna."

Anna was a great executive assistant. She always exemplified professionalism. Today was no exception. She operated with a high level of confidentiality and kept her on-point daily. Anna too was an immigrant but from El Salvador. She was able to escape the brutality that its citizens were experiencing—miraculously. Having worked for a wealthy businessman, Anna was able to get all of her travel documents within thirty days, including a ticket to the U.S. for herself and her mother. She was grateful.

She softly said to Ms. Yazzie, "You need to call Corey." Anna had been privy to Mia's personal life due to the nature of her job. At this moment she knew that she should step in to help Mia bring some balance to the moment.

Mia hesitated. "I'm not sure if he will be in agreement with the idea."

She paused before contacting him.

Anna said, "Perhaps not, but you need to tell him. Wasn't he scheduled to come down to Artesia in a few days?" She walked out of the room.

Mia called Corey. No answer.

She tried again. No answer.

At this juncture, she was concerned. Her thoughts began to race out of control. Corey owned a prestigious and successful company. He had to manage several employees to make sure that the company maintained its status. A man of his stature was not going to be available 24/7.

Later in the afternoon, Corey returned her call. She was slightly annoyed about the delay but knew that it was not a fair assessment of the situation. Mia told Corey about her assignment to go to Dubai by the weekend—the same weekend that he had planned to visit.

"Dubai, Mia? Why you?" he asked, sounding upset. "Sorry I wasn't available earlier when you called. I was in several meetings with some potential partners, but I *do* try to avail myself to you as much as possible. I know this is a requirement, I suppose, which come from your CEO, but I don't feel right. What happens now with our plans for this weekend?"

"One moment, Corey. Please," she said. Mia felt ill for a brief moment, not knowing what had brought on the flushed feeling and slight dizziness.

"Um, Corey. Let me call you back when I get home. I was just about to leave the office," she implored.

"Yes, Mia," he said with great uncertainty and hung up. *What is going on here?* Mia's behavior was troubling to him.

She called for Anna to pour her a glass of water. She felt perhaps she was feeling the symptoms of a flu or something. Anna offered to drive her home. They were both quiet on the way. After greeting Hadash, Mia went directly to her room, closed the door, and called Corey.

He was able to share his view on the matter. He explained to her that from a safety standpoint, she should not travel overseas alone. Mia clarified to him that Anna would also travel with her.

He wasn't satisfied with this arrangement either. "Two young attractive women, traveling alone? Not good!" had been his reply during their conversation. He told Mia that he will travel with them, if necessary.

In the meantime, she thought to lie down a bit, thinking that exhaustion affects the body in many different ways. She drifted off to sleep.

Hadash checked on her and decided not to awaken her for dinner.

The next morning, Mia went to the office feeling refreshed. She spoke with Les about Corey traveling with her and Anna.

"As long as he takes care of his own expenses, I don't have an issue with it," replied Les.

"Well, certainly!" chimed in Mia. "I wouldn't expect any company to take care of his expenses," she said with a bit of arrogance.

"Then it is settled," Les said.

"As a final note, I will have my assistant book his room, and of course, Anna can book his flight. She can coordinate the arrangements with him." Mia was relieved by Les's favorable response.

The week went by quickly. The arrangement that Corey made with Anna was that he would meet them in Dallas since they would be flying nonstop from DFW to Dubai. The flight was scheduled to depart at noon, so he would be at the airport at eight in the morning to meet them.

As Hadash prepared everything for Mia's packing, she asked, "Are you okay? You seem a bit tired…even more than usual."

"I can assure you, Hadash, that I am fine," Mia answered with assurance, but Hadash knew that she wasn't well.

With packing all completed, the next morning a limo service hired by Choice Wells drove Mia and Anna to Roswell to fly out for Dallas, Texas. The company had arranged for an overnight stay in Dallas before flying out on Friday at noon to Dubai.

Anna and Mia rested after reaching Dallas and enjoyed a really nice dinner at the Grand Hyatt. How this time was welcomed by them both.

Corey checked in with them several times just to be sure that all was well. On Friday morning, they met him downstairs as the Hyatt is actually located within the airport. He did not have to go outside.

Seeing Corey was refreshing. It has been some time now. He embraced Mia with a greeting, as well as Anna. They were prechecked already and only needed to get their luggage checked, which was not an issue because they were flying business class. They were escorted afterward to the business class lounge to wait until boarding time. The three talked and ate a very tasty breakfast, except Mia only wanted tea.

Boarding time began an hour and a half before the flight was scheduled to depart, and they were escorted to their own private cabin. The aircraft was beautiful, and the amenities provided by the airline for the long flight were awesome: pajamas, house slippers, toiletries, a lounge on board. Anna was taken aback. She had never traveled first or business class before.

Finally, after everyone boarded, they took off, but within thirty minutes of takeoff an announcement came over the intercom that a mechanical issue had developed and as a result they would have to make an emergency landing. Everyone began to panic as they were instructed on how to brace themselves.

Corey's cabin was in front of Mia's and Anna's, so he did his best to check on them as much as possible. One of the attendants saw him get up by utilizing a special safety device. He was instructed to immediately be seated, which he reluctantly did.

The landing was frightening, loud, and jolting. Upon impact, Mia somehow received injuries on her right side and arm. Anna sustained emotional trauma only, and Corey seemed okay. He checked again on Mia as the doors of the plane opened and the medics rushed onboard.

"Our luggage," exclaimed Mia, as they were being hustled off the broken aircraft.

"Do not worry about it," one of the attendants told her. "It would be taken care of."

Both Anna and Mia had their handbags with them, and Corey his briefcase. The attendant assigned to them got their hand luggage from the overhead bins with the help of two others. Corey smiled as he observed the unusual favor extended to them.

All medics and attendants performed extremely efficiently as they rushed several passengers to nearby hospitals. Corey and Anna were allowed to ride in the ambulance with Mia.

After only about ten minutes they arrived at the ER, and Mia was given excellent care. Immediately, several nurses, medics, and two doctors were drawing blood, checking vitals, and setting up X-ray equipment. After about a two-hour wait, the doctors came into the area where Mia had been assigned. He asked what the relationship was of Corey and Anna to Mia. Family? Husband? Anna excused herself. Corey was asked to stay by the insistence of Mia.

The doctor revealed that she had three broken ribs, and interestingly enough, he seemed troubled after saying, "I am so sorry to inform you—" A nurse came in at that very moment and took Mia's hand.

The doctor continued, "The injury to your ribs was too stressful and traumatic for...I'm sorry." The doctor walked out seemingly overcome by emotion, and the nurse stayed.

"What was he trying to say, ma'am? *Please*, what is going on?" Corey asked intensely. The doctor's emotional display alarmed him. Mia was weeping and in shock. She didn't know what the doctor was trying to say and why he became so emotional, but it was obviously something very serious. Mia was frightened.

"I'm sorry, Ms. Yazzie. Did you not know that you were pregnant?"

"What?" Mia screamed. "No! No! No! It can't be!"

They both wept so loudly that Anna heard them and returned to the area to find out what was going on. She too wept when she heard the devastating news.

Dubai? Certainly not at this time, thought Anna. *We have experienced a tragedy.*

She prayed, "Lord, we need Your divine intervention right now. Bring comfort and clarity regarding this case. Help us through this. Without You we will not be able to go through this journey."

After two more days in the hospital, Mia was discharged, though the broken ribs were yet in the healing process. The doctor said that it could take up to three or more weeks for them to heal well.

Corey remained in the area for several days after locating a hotel of his preference at Roswell, New Mexico, where Mia and Anna departed from when they flew to DFW. He only spent time there in the evenings to sleep, but the remainder of his time was spent between the hospital and assisting Hadash with errands. The groceries needed to be replenished, so Corey offered to drive Hadash wherever she needed to go and help with the expenses.

"Oh no, sir. It is okay," she would respond when he offered to purchase food items. "Auntie has given me a budget. Thank you, sir, but I am okay."

He wasn't sure if he should pursue the issue, so he called Mia at the hospital and inquired, "How are you feeling today, my dear?"

Mia answered with reluctance, "Well, Corey, this is my second day here. I don't feel any different from when I was admitted. Lots of pain and emotional stress. And the grief is—" Her voice choked up, and she began to cry heaving sobs. The tears streaming down her face represented the pouring out of guilt and disappointment, even the embarrassment that she felt as a result of losing the baby and especially coming to the reality that she didn't even know that she was carrying a child.

She began to wonder, *How would Grannie Yazzie feel about me now?* This was what she had always tried to guard against with Melanie, Jessica, and Mia. Silently she whispered, "Lord God, please forgive me once more."

Mia did not know much about the power of repentance and the power of God's grace. She had already repented many times. When we call upon the Lord with a pure and sincere heart, He hears and He forgives. This is something about God's nature and sovereignty that she would come to know.

Corey tried to comfort her. "We will be okay, Mia. I honor you and I will show a measure of my honor by marrying you as promised. As soon as you are healed, we will get married. Messiah will strengthen you and me." He went on to say, "I have asked for forgiveness, and according to Rabbi Reuben's teaching last weekend, God is faithful and just to forgive us of our sins and cleanse us from all unrighteousness."

Mia was listening but was still disturbed about the loss of the baby.

"Corey, what do you think happens to a baby that is miscarried?" Mia allowed her most private contemplations to escape her lips.

"The baby is not at fault, Mia, and this is not your fault about the emergency plane landing. I have also learned that Messiah, our Lord, is sovereign. What we don't understand, He already does, and has plans to bring about healing and repentance to our hearts." Corey's answer was oddly comforting.

"Mia, I have learned over the past month and a half that God has a call upon my life and that I must be obedient to the call. Just rest. I will take Hadash to the market in a couple of hours, then I will come back to the hospital," he exhorted. "Can I get you anything?"

Stands With Arms Open smiled for the first time since tragedy struck. She wiped her tears while saying, "I am okay. I don't need anything at the moment." But then she paused and said, "Oh yes! I need a Bible please. Could you and Hadash find a place to purchase one for me?" she asked.

"Absolutely!" he responded. "See you soon."

About thirty minutes after speaking with Corey, a social worker walked into her private suite and asked if she was open to speak with a grief counselor from the chaplain's department. He went on to explain that in cases like hers, they provide this service. She nodded. "Yes."

The counselor visited Mia shortly afterward and just sat with her, holding her hands for a few minutes before speaking. These were the most powerful moments of silence that she had ever experienced. The conversation echoed what Corey had shared earlier. "Amazing," said Mia. "Thank you so much." The counselor told her that she was leaving some literature on the stand by the bed for her to read at her convenience.

*****

Hadash and Corey headed to the local farmer's market. In Artesia, being a small town with a population of a little under 12,000 people, locating a farmer's market was a no-brainer. Even though Hadash frequented the farmer's market to make purchases for the household, Corey wanted to take the lead locating one this time. Hadash had it in mind to prepare a special dinner for them both upon Mia's discharge later in the week, so she directed him where to go for what once they entered the grounds. Hadash had decided to prepare a special Sudanese dish, Goraasa be Dama. But she determined to substitute the stew beef with short ribs of beef. She would require tomatoes, cardamom, and cinnamon. She wasn't sure if she wanted to use cinnamon this time, though. Sage sounded like a better option. Certainly, she would add green chili—New Mexico's chili—which it is famously known for, and some red, yellow, and green bell peppers. How appetizing. Mia loved fresh-cut green beans from the market. That was settled. But she was not certain what Corey liked to eat, so she asked him if he had any special requests.

He answered, "Red chili on the side."

"No problem, sir," responded Hadash. She was thinking of a bread. Perhaps she could make a flatbread batter native to Sudan. Hadash accessed the menu and stopped to think.

"Oh, sorry, sir, but can you get some brown rice for me?"

Eager to be of help, Corey went out and about the large market with its appetizing sights and sounds, searching for brown rice. Hadash slightly chuckled as he took off.

After loading up with lots of veggies, fruits, seasonings and grains, preserves and jellies, they checked out and headed home, except on the way back, Corey recalled that he needed to purchase a Bible for Mia first.

"I know just the place," offered Hadash. "At the second light, turn right, and only a little way down we will see a small Bible store." As Corey turned the corner, Hadash pointed, "There it is!"

Corey browsed for a moment, admitting that it was his very first time visiting a Bible store. So many different types of Bibles and study helps were available, as well as biographies. *So much,* he thought. The rabbi at Bet Temple had given Corey a Jewish Bible upon his first visit. He cherished it.

They returned home where Corey assisted with removing groceries from the vehicle, then informed Hadash that he would be heading back to the hospital to visit with Mia for the remainder of the day.

The visit was good. Mia was in much better spirits. Corey was pleased. He returned to Roswell at six in the evening not only to rest but to do some work on his computer. A conference call with the board had been scheduled for six thirty. He cancelled and rescheduled for the next morning.

Assisting Hadash and visiting Mia continued until she was discharged and settled at home. The special meal was prepared on the day of Mia's return home. The aromas were beyond description. Before completing the meal, Hadash prepared Mia's room by vacuuming, sanitizing everything, dusting, and changing the bedding on her beautiful queen-sized bed with its crushed velvet headboard.

Bright colorful sheets and pillowcases would be ideal, Hadash mused. "Everything must be fresh and clean for Auntie," she said aloud.

Dinner was served at five in the afternoon. Mia was welcomed home by dozens of cards, several balloons, and flowers, flowers, flowers—everywhere she looked, there were flowers. Each day as she was recovering at the hospital, office staff, friends, and members of her new church family came by to show their love and concern. Their tokens of love warmed Mia's heart.

*****

"What a delicious meal," said Corey. "I mean, this was amazing!" Mia joined him with giving accolades to Hadash. She and Corey asked for one more round of seconds.

Hadash always replied, "You are welcome. Please, Auntie…please, sir, enjoy your food. You must eat well, Mia. You need your strength." She brooded over them like a mother hen to make sure they were okay.

Corey returned to the hotel and asked Hadash to take good care of Mia. "See to it that she has her meds on time and call me if anything. I will need to work from the hotel tomorrow but will be back the day after."

Hadash briefly bowed as she said, "Certainly, sir. Good night, sir."

Mia had retired prior to the conversation. She was extremely pleased with the brightness of the bedding and, of course, more flowers.

A few days later Corey returned to Mia's home after having Anna to join them to begin making plans for March 9, 2018.

"What time?" asked Anna.

"At 3:00 p.m. before Shabbat. My rabbi will officiate, along with Mia's new pastor.

CHAPTER 9

REMEMBERING TAOS

Mia awakened on a weekend night after returning from the hospital to very loud claps of thunder and a steady sound of a rain downpour. She looked at her clock radio. It was 10:20 p.m. Lightning was flashing every few seconds, and she noticed that her bedroom blinds had not been drawn. Her home decor specialist had introduced her to a style of drapery which blended the heavy blinds with curtains made of sheer material. Rather than having the two separately, it is woven into one. They were beautiful and, of course, in Mia's favorite light-turquoise color.

The rain was relaxing, but the thunder and lightning were quite intimidating.

During her childhood, Mia and her sisters would hide under their bed covers during a thunderstorm, sometimes laughing about how afraid they were as the three of them snuggled under blankets and quilts. They never knew as children what it meant to be able to have their own rooms. It would be years before that luxury would become a reality.

Each morning, they would collect firewood from the woodshed that was covered with quilts and plastics to protect it from rain and snow. Grannie would insist that they collect the wood by five in the morning so that the stove could be well heated to prepare breakfast and keep the adobe warm.

When all was ready, Grannie Yazzie, Melanie, Jessica, and Mia would all sit down to a hearty breakfast of red beans, sometimes sausage, home-fried potatoes, and tortillas cooked on the potbelly stove. There were no ovens on the reservation that used electricity or gas for cooking, but Grannie always reminded them that they should be grateful for what they had.

Watching television when there was an opportunity, they saw how other kids lived with their beautiful bedrooms, kitchen appliances, convenient toilet areas, and private bathrooms—not outside or not set up as an attachment to their homes. They longed for those days to come for them!

Grannie would notice them watching with intensity and a deep longing in their eyes. She would walk in and out of the room and say, "Be grateful for what you have," often in a Navajo dialect. They didn't speak the dialect or language very much, but they knew what she meant.

The rain and claps of thunder did not let up for hours. Briefly, while trying to go back to sleep, she thought she heard Hadash moving about in the kitchen. Mia carefully eased off the bed into her satin, feathery slippers, grabbed her robe, and opened her bedroom door while slightly tying the belt of the robe.

She called out, "Hadash?"

Hadash quickly emerged from the kitchen into the hall and asked, "Auntie, are you okay? Do you need something?"

Mia answered, "I am fine. Just checking on you. Are there candles that you can light if the electricity goes out? I don't think we will need to turn on the generator."

"Don't worry, Auntie. It is okay. Do you want a nice cup of peppermint tea? You really shouldn't be out of bed. You are still trying to gain your strength back."

"Yes, thanks, I would like some tea," Mia answered, as she reflected upon the cups of tea and hot chocolate that Mrs. Garcia would serve at The Place B&B in Taos, New Mexico, gourmet breakfasts in the mornings, and on Friday afternoons, hot tea and cookies. Mia enjoyed the experience. Mrs. Garcia would deliver breakfast, but due to lack of staff by afternoon on days with heavy snow, the anticipated serving of tea and cookies would not be available. The bed-and-breakfast was uniquely designed such as to allow the staff to deliver meals under a protective covering. Many guests dine in the common area, which was cozy and beautifully decorated. Mia opted to have her meals delivered to her when available.

Though Mia had a double fireplace in her bedroom at home that warmed the bedroom from one angle and the bath area from another angle, she, for some reason, especially enjoyed the fireplace in her suite at the bed-and-breakfast in Taos.

She reflected upon the many days that she would sit, relaxing at the bay window to watch the snow falling and people moving about on the sidewalks. Some people appeared to have been gift shopping, others stepping into the local bakery across the street from her vantage point. Cars and trucks, mainly, would pass by slowly but only a few.

Taos, being situated at an almost seven-thousand-foot elevation with a population in 2017 of about 5,688 people, according to the census, consists of an almost equal blend of Native Americans, Spanish, and European cultures. Taos is a beautiful diversified town. It was a city that Mia often read about in tour books and on the Internet. In 2014, she knew that she would someday visit this intriguing place, but she was not being drawn there as an artist as many, many people are, but as a tourist. She had spent many moments thinking of how special it would be to spend Christmas there and to experience it in the winter season.

A knock on the door interrupted Mia's deep thoughts and reminiscing about Taos.

"Mia," Hadash said as she knocked, "I have your tea."

"Please, Hadash, come in."

Hadash set the tea on the nightstand and, bowing, said, "Please, Auntie, drink your tea and sleep please. I beg you."

"I will," responded Mia. "I promise."

The tea was delicious and welcomed. *Now to try to rest,* she thought upon finishing. A loud clap of thunder, preceded by an electric bolt of lightning that lit up the sky, jolted Mia away from her intentions of sleeping. She pulled out her nightstand drawer to look for her cell phone.

Where is my phone? she asked herself with a puzzled feeling, as she tossed this and that aside to find it. *I need to listen to some Bible scriptures or worship music…something!* She had an intense hunger for something spiritual. Forget her PC. It was at the office. She didn't find the phone and concluded she had left it in the kitchen area. She did not feel inclined to get up to look for it, and Mia resigned herself to getting it in the morning.

"Okay," the restless Mia decided. "I will try to lie down and sleep again."

Mia eventually dozed off and slept to the drumbeat of the constant downpour of rain and, by now, the sounds of distant thunder. She again dreamed that she and Corey got married at a romantic ceremony in idyllic Taos. It was so breathtaking, so euphoric, so real!

She awakened in good spirits with many thoughts about the dream. *I wonder,* she mused, *if this will actually become a reality?* Perhaps she could return to Taos and stay at her favorite bed-and-breakfast. *It would be great,* she thought, *to see Mrs. Garcia again and enjoy some of the sites in Taos that I wasn't able to experience in the winter.*

Taos, the oldest pueblo community situated in New Mexico, draws many tourists yearly, along with artists who have become residents there.

Getting married in Taos would be an experience beyond experiences.

The rain had stopped, the storm had passed, a new day was before Mia. Now to continue relaxing, reading, praying, and looking forward to what the future held in store for her.

CHAPTER 10

✳

A TAOS WEDDING

Mia was feeling much stronger as her broken ribs were mending quickly, according to her last X-Ray.

She was up to meeting with Corey and Anna to discuss wedding plans. The three were sitting in the family room holding initial discussions. They got to a point where they needed to make a decision regarding a venue. It was agreed that Anna would be the one to check for a restaurant that displayed a Spanish archway. Mia remembered where she had seen one before and asked Corey, "Could we return to the restaurant in Taos where we had Christmas dinner? It had a lovely Spanish archway."

"Mia, whatever you wish. Anna, check with The Love Apple in Taos for us. Include everything needed…flowers…well, just hire a wedding planner and you direct her or him with the particulars," he explained.

"Excuse me, Mr. Hartman. If I might interject here. But I think we need to also connect Mia with the wedding planner to discuss colors and number of guests."

"Absolutely," he responded, rising from his seat. Corey had to run. He needed to get to the airport quickly to catch a flight. He kissed Mia goodbye, charging her to rest, and left all plans in Anna's hands. She was to involve Mia to determine what her wishes might be moving forward.

*****

A few days had passed, and Anna called Hadash to check on Mia and to see when she might feel up to sitting with her for about thirty minutes. Anna waited on the line; Hadash returned on a positive note. Mia had invited Anna to come by for dinner and suggested that they overlap the wedding meeting at that time. Anna was elated.

Since they were having a guest for dinner, Hadash changed her planned menu to a comforting meatball veggie soup, albondigas soup, sopapillas, and iced tea.

Mia rested and read her Bible most of the day. She had even reached a point where she wasn't concerned about office activities anymore. She determined to truly rest, but now with her wedding on the horizon, she would need to shift her concentration toward one of the most important days of her life.

Anna arrived by five thirty in the afternoon. Dinner was served right away as they pored over wedding logistics.

Mia said with a hint of regret, "I don't think it would be okay to have a large celebration knowing that I don't deserve it—"

"Mia, no!" Anna immediately rebuffed Mia's train of thought. "Don't think that way! You can have a large celebration if you want to."

"No, I am convicted about this. I only want you, Hadash, my sister Jessica—we would have to locate her—my immediate office staff, and two ladies that I recently met at the church," she said emphatically.

"What of Corey's family?" Anna asked.

"I don't know them. We would have to ask Corey."

Anna promptly picked up her phone to call Corey. No time to waste!

"Mr. Hartman. Are there any members of your family who you would like to be in attendance at the wedding?"

Corey's response was instant. "Without a doubt, my parents. We must book their tickets from Frankfurt straightaway. I have been in touch with them, though I haven't mentioned it to Mia as yet. They will definitely attend." Mia was happy to hear that. She looked forward to meeting them.

Mia and Anna continued pulling bits and pieces of the wedding plans together until the official wedding planner got there. He was on his way. Once he arrived everything moved along smoothly. The Love Apple was booked, flower arrangements were set, colors of turquoise and silver were chosen. It was going to be a Taos wedding—Mia's Taos wedding!

*****

Plans quickly came together while, at the same time, Mia's recovery continued to improve. She thought of her sister Jessica often, especially from the moment of the flight accident until now. She called her. No answer. She tried again. No answer.

Is Jessica avoiding me? she wondered. Mia didn't blame her if she was, considering their last conversation.

Finally, Jessica called back. Mia was ecstatic—relieved even—to see Jessica's name on the caller ID. She answered the call immediately. Mia apologized for not helping her when she needed it. They talked for about an hour. Jessica was very sorry to hear about Mia's loss. They cried together then truly reconciled. Mia invited Jessica and her five children to the wedding with, of course, all expenses paid. Mia *really* wanted her sister there to be a part of her special day.

The days leading up to the wedding went by very quickly. Mia even went to the office a few times just to stay in touch with the staff and to keep the company moving forward.

So much excitement was developing at the office with Mia's friends and her sister. Hadash and Anna were extremely busy working with Pierre, the wedding planner, who had moved to New Mexico only two years prior from France. He brought a Parisian flare to the planning table. Every detail was being exquisitely designed.

Mia wanted a flute player to perform before she entered and following the reciting of the vows.

The next really important detail was her dress, which should have been the first item following the date being set. Mia wanted a simple, fitted, A-line dress that fell just below the knee. "A hint of beaded turquoise would also be nice, Manuel." Her eyes glistened with glee as she communicated her wishes to the dressmaker. Mia was sure of his ability to deliver what she envisioned. His reputation was far-reaching.

"No problem," Manuel responded with a contagious exuberance. "This dress will be gorgeous on you."

Anna volunteered to shop for shoes.

"I already have my shoes, Anna. I just need jewelry."

Anna was quick on the ball to offer to fulfill that task. She was almost as excited about the wedding as Mia was. Everything began to fall into place. March 9 would soon be here.

Corey's parents arrived two days before the wedding, and Jessica, a day before. Getting all of her children prepared for travel was not an easy task.

On March 8, Mia and Corey and members of the wedding party set out to travel to Taos in luxurious limos from Artesia and Albuquerque. Family members were being chauffeured by limousine as well. Their destination was The Place B&B, which Mia enjoyed so much during her three-week leave for Christmas.

As they left Mia's home, Pierre and Anna reassured them that everything had been prepared and was just awaiting their arrival. Everyone breathed a sigh of relief. Corey and Mia laid their heads against the back of the seat and said, "Finally!"

Corey had made all the transportation arrangements, placing himself and Mia in the same car with his parents so that they could get acquainted with each other.

The driver spoke through an intercom system, "There is champagne and sodas, as well as water there in the cooler."

Corey thanked him, but everyone only drank water. A disclaimer had been established on the invitations that *no* alcoholic beverages will be served prior to, during, nor after any of the wedding festivities. Pierre was not okay with this, but he was hired to fulfill the wishes of the bride and groom, so he gave in to their request, however reluctantly.

Arriving in Taos was a delight. A bit of snow still remained on the mountains; after all, this was Taos, New Mexico, and just early March.

When they entered The Place B&B, a local caterer was waiting for everyone in Mia's suite. Mia wanted to see Mrs. Garcia but learned that she had retired.

Fancy hor d'oeuvres were displayed along with a beautiful fruit presentation and barbecue winglets. The spread was both breathtaking and delicious. Topping it off was a fruit punch fountain—*so elegant.*

Everyone decided to rest after sharing a fun time of meet-and-greet at the pre-wedding reception. Each of the guests were escorted to their suites.

Sleep was welcomed. It had been a busy few weeks of preparation. Corey called Mia from his suite and encouraged her to rest and soothed any last-minute jitters. "It would be a great day," he reassured her, "and I am looking forward to spending the rest of my life with you." Corey cleared his throat. "I love you, Ms. Mia Yazzie… soon-to-be Mrs. Mia Hartman."

It had a nice ring to it. Mia blushed. His words moved her.

"I love you too, Corey…with all my heart." Her voice was tender and sincere. He knew she meant it.

There was a momentary silence as they both took it all in, enraptured by the reality of their affection for each other.

Corey broke the silence. "Good night, Stands With Arms Open."

"Good night, Corey."

*****

The morning was filled with having a light breakfast and finishing up last-minute details. Pierre, Anna, and now Hadash made trips to the wedding location to ensure that everything was in order.

Corey spent time with his parents, and they also took some time getting to know Mia. It was an easy flowing exchange, and they concluded that their son had made a great choice.

A little later in the day, Mia and Jessica also took some time to bond. These were memorable and precious moments filled with lots of laughter.

Mid-laugh, Jessica looked at her watch.

"Mia! It's time for you to get ready! You can't be late for your own wedding!"

"No, I can't!" Mia shot to her feet. She and Jessica hugged each other, and then they both ran off to their respective rooms. It was *really* time.

*****

At one thirty in the afternoon, the limos returned to chauffeur the wedding party, which now included Rabbi Reuben and Pastor Trujillo, Mia's pastor. Corey treated everyone royally. They were both excited and blessed to be among such a beautiful couple and family members. Upon arrival at their destination, the restaurant staff met Pierre and gave him instructions regarding the setup. The restaurant had two available rooms for everyone to wait until it was time to come out. The wedding took place in the open around the Spanish archway; the weather was good. Pierre had so creatively arranged for chairs to be decorated; it was just beyond exquisite. He had also organized for the entire restaurant to be used for the wedding, which wasn't a major problem since they opened for dinner at five in the afternoon anyway. A quarter before three, everyone was in place, and at three o'clock Mia walked down an aisle leading to the Spanish archway. She looked absolutely stunning as she walked gracefully in her silver-beaded turquoise dress, with a bouquet of roses, orchids, and a few carnations in hand. She remembered that Grannie had said she would one day meet a wealthy man from the West, and he would marry her. Grannie Yazzie was right! The day had come!

Contemporary music playing in the background, preceded by a Native flute player, was more than anyone could describe. The couple prepared their own vows, and the rabbi and pastor incorporated a bit of Jewish and Christian traditions into the ceremony. The creativity of this wedding was like nothing that either spiritual leader had *ever* experienced before nor the members of the wedding party.

The uniqueness of the music caught the attention of the restaurant staff.

The ceremony concluded with the traditional finale where the groom salutes his bride with a kiss and the officiant pronounces them husband and wife, and it was so.

"Mr. and Mrs. Corey Hartman!"

Cheers erupted from those present. Even the restaurant staff joined in.

The flute player performed once more, and the happy couple walked together from under the Spanish archway. Arm in arm and with their faces ablaze with bright smiles, both Corey and Mia recalled how awed they were at the ambiance of the Spanish archway during their date at The Love Apple last Christmas; right then and there, they believed that they would one day stand in this very spot as a couple. Their dream had come true.

After the ceremony, the wedding party and guests all greeted each other and joyfully congratulated the newlywed couple standing at the end of the wedding aisle runner. Corey and his new bride were taking the time to mingle a bit with his parents, Jessica, and Mia's friends, when the photographer called them all together for group shots to immortalize the momentous occasion.

Anna made sure that all post-wedding details were managed, including transport to The Place B&B and trips back to Artesia.

Goodbyes were sweet and very special. Pierre was commended on doing a splendid job. The pastor and rabbi exchanged farewells.

Mia and Corey stepped into a decorated limo, waved goodbye to everyone, and headed to Santa Fe for their honeymoon. Mia would have an opportunity to experience a stay at a hacienda that she had so yearned for.

Leaving Taos brought back such great memories. One of the most memorable times of her life would always be the winter days that she spent in Taos, New Mexico.

Now on to building new unforgettable moments with the love of her life.

ABOUT THE AUTHOR

D r. Elizabeth Hairston-McBurrows has authored several books, including *Gates of Freedom*, *Apostolic Intervention*, *Go Forth in Dance*, and *Taos Winter* (a romance novel). She has also had the distinct honor of being recognized and awarded by a number of world leaders for her profound contribution to society. In 2004, Dr. Hairston-McBurrows received a Letter of Recognition as a Global Leader by the then President of the United States, Mr. George W. Bush. In September 2007, she was appointed Ambassador to the Ivory Coast by the Autorités Consulaires do la Côte d'Ivoire, an affiliate of the President and government of the Ivory Coast, West Africa, and in 2011, Dr. McBurrows was the recipient of an Outstanding Citizen Award by the State of New Mexico African American Affairs in the area of Education. Most notably, in September 2015, the Interfaith Peace-Building Initiative of the North American Division to the United Nations, New York, presented her with the Golden Rule International Award.

Dr. Elizabeth pursued studies in multiple areas and has a Bachelor of Arts degree in English Literature, with a minor in Speech and Drama, as well as a Master of Arts and a Master of Fine Arts in Christian Education and Drama.

At the doctoral level, Dr. Hairston-McBurrows earned a Doctorate of Biblical Studies degree from International Seminary, Plymouth, Florida; in addition to a Doctorate of Divinity Degree and a PhD from Friends International University, Merced, California. She also served as an Adjunct Professor and faculty member of Friends International.

Dr. Elizabeth gave up a career in show business to become an Ambassador for Jesus Christ. In 1987, the late Archbishop Benson Idahosa of Benin, Nigeria, West Africa, ordained Dr. Hairston-McBurrows for the gospel ministry. In 1997, she made history by being the first woman ordained to the office of Apostle under the Christian International Network by Apostolic-Bishop Dr. Bill Hamon.

Dr. Hairston-McBurrows ministers prophetically and apostolically in music, dance, and drama and teaches the Word of God in a relevant, simple, yet revelatory and uncompromising way. She has also been graced with opportunities to minister the Word of the Lord to presidents, prime ministers, and kings in various foreign countries. Apostle McBurrows is a leader of leaders who presently serves as Founding President of The Apostolic-Prophetic Connection, Inc. (a ministry that bridges the gap between the fivefold and the arts) and is International President and Founder of Women With a Call International, Inc., with branches in nations around the world, including the United States of America, Holland, Africa, India, and Japan, among others.

Dr. Elizabeth has also had the esteemed privilege of serving as a radio show host before crossing the media bridge to actively pursue the role of TV talk show host on several television networks. She has personally produced, filmed, and hosted a magazine talk show, *Women With a Call*, and was a featured guest on *Dancing Preachers Reality Show*, Impact Television Network. She is an actress and model and has been allocated parts in films, ads, and other broadcast presentations. The Internet has enlarged her possibilities even further, and she is a podcast host with Charisma Media.

Dr. Hairston-McBurrows currently resides in Central New Mexico with her husband, Dr. Carlton McBurrows, and has two beautiful daughters, Constance and CharÉ.

Viga ceilings
garlic keeps your heart
from beating fast q.q.
Sangre Christo Mountains

CPSIA information can be obtained
at www.ICGtesting.com
Printed in the USA
BVHW041528131221
623936BV00012B/407

9 781638 855170